OLEANDER - DARK SOLAR TRILOGY - BOOK 1

D.N. LEO

EXCLUSIVE INVITATION

DARK SOLAR TRILOGY

DARK SOLAR TRILOGY
by D.N Leo

OLEANDER
WOLFSBANE
MAIKOA

Dark Solar Trilogy - By D.N. Leo

PART I

PROLOGUE

Some rise by sin, and some by virtue fall.
William Shakespeare

Scotland, 1864

*C*harmine brushed her hand over the tips of the cold, wet grass as she sauntered along a narrow path that led to a small bush off the rolling hillside. She inhaled deeply. She liked the feel of the chilled winter air rushing through every cell in her body. It was as pure and clear as crystal, she thought. Where she came from, there was no such thing as what they called "the weather" here, and there was certainly no winter. Everything in her world was perfectly controlled—it was a world of purity. She laughed when she heard people on Earth refer to her world as Heaven. The name did have a nice ring to it. But for some reason, she didn't appreciate that world as much as Jael did.

Her beloved husband was the righteous angel of light, but she was only an apprentice-to-be in the house of Gods. She was on maternity leave from a job she hadn't yet gotten when she became pregnant. She had become so bored in that perfect world of hers that she'd pressured her husband to let her go with him on a mission to Earth. She'd been with him to many places, but Earth was her favorite.

She rubbed absently at her tummy. It would be a while before she showed any sign of pregnancy, but Jael didn't like her hanging around the house of Gods while she was with child. He suspected there was a dirty angel in his council—someone who had been dealing with the dark side.

Aren't angels supposed to be the most righteous of the righteous? she thought, but as she had done several times before, she brushed that thought aside. She knew her husband well. He didn't have the evidence to support his accusation and would keep it to himself for the safety of her and their first child.

From her bag, she pulled out a newly released novel she had just bought from a merchant on the main street in town. She rubbed her thumb along the spine of the book and sniffed the pages. She loved the smell of Earth paper. Jael would probably laugh at her sentiment when she gave the book to him tonight, but she loved the story. It was a fairy tale—one that was so close to their own story. She would never forget the look in Jael's eyes when they got married by the lake. They didn't need any approval. All they ever needed was their love for each other.

Charmine frowned when she looked down and saw the bunch of wild roses in front of her suddenly turn from blood red to snow white. She shook her head to clear her vision. Then she watched as the roses returned to their deep red hue again. But before she could feel any relief at the change, she heard a bone-chilling chuckle from behind her.

She knew that sound well.

For more than five years, she had not heard it, and she wished the situation had stayed that way.

She turned around.

In front of her was the magnificent angel of ice. Her long white hair flew in the wind, and her porcelain skin was so perfectly white that it looked as if she had no blood flowing through her body. Angel of ice was not an official position—Charmine had given her sister that name because she was as cold and heartless as a piece of ice.

"Luna," Charmine said, keeping her voice as calm as possible. Her sister was the best student of dark magic and could do things beyond imagination. Charmine knew for certain that the very moment she showed weakness, Luna would attack her. She also knew Luna didn't read minds, so she did her best to keep her fear at bay.

"Well, long time no see, sister. I didn't know your husband took you on a mission with him. You're barely an apprentice. What can you possibly do to help him?"

She shrugged and asked, "What do you want?"

Luna laughed. "Oh dear sister, why do you always assume I want something from you?"

"Because you always do."

Luna nodded and walked slowly in a circle, her eyes measured. "Perhaps you're right. But you wouldn't give me what I want, so I'll save my breath and just tell you straight out—I have Jael." Luna stared at her.

Charmine felt as if her world was tumbling down. She knew Luna was serious, but part of her wanted to deny what was happening. She knew Luna was here because she hadn't gotten *all* she wanted.

Luna threw a bloody feather on the ground, her eyebrow arching as she waited for Charmine's reaction.

Charmine smiled. "The last time I saw Jael spreading his wings, they were magnificent. He might have shed a few feathers here and there. So you want me to believe you have him just because you grabbed a loose feather? I don't have magical power, but I do have a good brain, Luna. And that feather tells me nothing." She put up a brave front, but on the inside, her world had totally collapsed. The only way an angel like her husband would let anyone get to his wings was if he were dead.

"I have no intention of convincing you."

"Then don't. You're wasting my time."

Luna shook her head. "I am here to take what's mine."

"I owe you nothing."

"Oh, yes, you do. Jael chose you over me, and I don't like being rejected. You see, there is nothing you have that I don't—"

"A heart," Charmine cut in.

Luna laughed. "Right, again, sister. To focus on my magic, I had to let go of that silly human sentiment. But I still need men to satisfy my basic needs." Her eyes darkened as she approached Charmine. "There will be severe consequences for refusing me. You're smart, you know that, right?"

Charmine backed away. "If you need sex, find a brothel. If you need love, then you at least need a heart that functions as more than just a mere organ. Killing me isn't going to solve any of your problems."

"Blood is thicker than water, Charmine. If I wanted you dead, you wouldn't be standing here."

Charmine backed up into to a tree. "You want to hurt me with something worse than death..."

Luna smirked. "Yes, I want your child." Luna reached her hands out to grab Charmine's shoulders.

Charmine couldn't back away any further. "Over my dead body," she said and turned to run.

Luna turned, and her arms reached out like two gigantic snakes. Her hands grabbed the back of Charmine's coat, pulling her back.

Charmine swung her arm and whacked the spine of the book she was holding against Luna's face, hitting her in between her eyes. The book dropped to the ground.

Luna staggered back and growled. She picked up the book and glanced at the cover. "You hit me with a fairy tale?"

"If you know what it is, there's still hope for you. Why are you doing this, Luna?"

Luna growled and pushed Charmine to the ground on her back-side. When Luna approached, Charmine stomped a kick at her abdomen, sending her evil sister to the ground.

Charmine scrambled to her feet and ran. But she had taken only a few steps before she felt Luna's hands grab her ankles, tripping her to the ground. She fell face down, hitting her head hard. She yanked her legs from Luna's hands, scrambled up, and ran again.

"Do *not* walk away from me. *Nobody* walks away from me!" Luna yelled.

But Charmine kept running until she felt Luna's hand shove at her back. She fell again. Because of her momentum, this fall was hard, and she couldn't get back up. She turned around. Seeing Luna approaching, she pushed herself with her legs, sliding backward on the ground. Then she hit a large rock and couldn't back away any further.

Luna crouched. "We're sisters. I don't want to kill you or hurt you in any way. I just want to share my life with you. You have Jael. You're carrying his child. Now we can share that. Blood is thicker than water after all."

Tears streamed down Charmine's face. "I am sharing nothing with you," she said.

She saw Luna pull out a knife, and she kicked out hard at her, but her sister caught her right ankle. Her hands were as unyielding as steel, and her fingers dug into Charmine's flesh. Luna twisted her hands. Charmine could feel her flesh and tendons tear, and her bones shatter. The pain invaded her brain. Amid the haze of excruciating agony, she kept her mind clear. She would never give in to evil. She would never disappoint her husband.

Her body was paralyzed, and her mind started to go numb. Without saying a word, she stared at Luna in challenge.

"I can see you're a tough one as well. It's good for the child." Luna chuckled. She cut her own hand, and a smile spread across her face as she watched the blood seeping out. She grabbed Charmine's hand, slashed a deep cut in her palm, and pressed their wounds together.

What erupted from Luna's mouth was not her own voice but a deep, croaking, evil sound. "We now share the child. With all the mighty power of the darkness, let the child have all of my magic, all the light of the father, and all the wits of the mother. This child will be the best of all devils. But the child shall have no heart."

Charmine screamed. With all the strength she had left, she

yanked the knife out of Luna's hand and stabbed it deep into her sister's heart.

Luna froze and looked at Charmine. She had stopped chanting the curse, but she was about to move again. Charmine pulled the knife back out and plunged it into her sister again.

Then Charmine crawled away, her injured leg dragging behind.

Luna let out a haunting sound. She looked to the sky, her arms wide open, and her eyes blank. From her open mouth, toxic fumes spewed out. The surrounding trees and grass died instantly.

And all Charmine saw after that was darkness.

a large group of well-dressed citizens crowded together in front of the Metropolitan Symphony Center. The group was being held back by first grade guards. In Iilos, a small dimension of the multiverse, first grade guards dealt with civilians. Seeing the commotion at the bottom of the hill, Dinah shook her head, feeling pity for the guards. She couldn't imagine herself doing such a boring job, regardless of how much she was paid for it.

She didn't know what the dispute was about, but she hoped the show was still on. She had been waiting for this musical for a long time, and it hadn't been easy to get tickets. Well, admittedly, it wasn't she who had gotten the tickets. Her girlfriend, Kate, had worked her magic again. Kate had a way with men when she needed to get things done. And Dinah admired her for that.

She hadn't been in Iilos for long, but she liked this dimension. It had been founded by Moira LeBlanc, a citizen of a country on Earth called Ireland. History suggested that Moira had replicated a model of her homeland in this dimension, and that was why its facade was that of the Irish countryside. But unlike Ireland, the technology that powered this universe was one of the most advanced in the cosmos.

What she liked most about Iilos was that the citizens here were mostly human-like, and English was the official language.

Iilos had never been open to those from other universes. But when Moira passed, her daughter had opened the dimension to receive new citizens—those with skills—from other universes. Dinah was one of the skilled migrants.

She didn't have to migrate. She was a licensed freelance private investigator. She could travel across the multiverse already, using a professional pass issued by the Daimon Gate. But there was something about Iilos that appealed to her, and so she had decided to officially migrate and call Iilos home.

"Ouch!" she said as one of her pointy heels got stuck in a crack in the pavement, throwing her body forward. She fell hard against a low brick wall, stopping her fall with her palms to prevent an ugly face-planting incident. "Damn," she said when she looked at her palm and saw that a bruise had already started to form. At least she hadn't broken any bones. Kate called her a klutz for very good reasons.

"I'm not a klutz. It's these stupid heels. I hate them!" she muttered to herself. She barely hit five foot two. People always said good things came in small packages. But she didn't believe that to be true in her case. She wore high heels to compensate for her lack in height, but she much preferred her chunky platform boots to these pointy heels because it was easier to hide lethal weapons in them. Her appearance and outfits had landed her a portfolio of high-action cases. Well, *high-action* was her term. Cooper, her business partner, called them violent cases.

Her wrist unit buzzed. "Engage," she said. On the screen, Cooper came on. *Speak of the devil*, she thought.

Cooper blinked his striking blue eyes, looked at her with a grin, and held a flask up to the screen.

"No, Cooper, the compound needs to stay in the flask for one more day."

"I think it's ready. I'm going to try it."

"Don't you dare. If you mess up my experiment, I'll tell your girl-friend your abs are fake."

Cooper frowned. "That's a nasty threat!"

"You didn't work for those muscles! You used my chemical! As far as I'm concerned, they're fake. But that's not why you called. So what do you want?"

"There's a job in Xiilok—"

"No, Cooper. We talked about this. We don't take jobs from Xiilok."

"But this one is easy, and it's lucrative."

"You can take it, but I won't."

"We're pals, Dinah. Come on...help me out. It's just a delivery. It's easy. But on the delivery end, the chemical has to be put together, and I don't know jack about chemicals."

"What kind of chemical?"

Cooper rolled his eyes. "If I knew the answer to that question, would I be asking you? I have the specs of the merchandise. Do you mind taking a quick look and seeing if we can handle it? It pays thirty thousand credits."

"How much?"

"See, I told you it's lucrative."

"There has to be a catch. Why us? We're not known for delivering merchandise."

"It's not the delivery...it's the *assembly*. They said they need someone who knows chemicals. And you do have a reputation for that."

"Let me think about it."

"Oh, come on! I'll give you seventy percent of the fees. I'll buy you breakfast every day for a whole year. I'll—"

"I said I'll think about it. I'll get back to you tomorrow, okay?"

"Promise? It's important. I need ten thousand credits, Dinah. I need them."

"Why? You don't need many credits to live in Iilos."

"A guy I know found a way to migrate to Eudaiz."

"What's wrong with Iilos?"

"Nothing. But Eudaiz is everyone's dream. Don't you want to live there?"

"I don't daydream. Plus, Eudaiz doesn't take people based on wealth."

"I know. So when this guy finds a way, it costs."

"He's conning you."

"Well, I don't want to have regrets for not trying. I'll see you tomorrow?"

"Okay. Yes, Cooper." She hung up. A group of women walked past her. One of them was more than six feet tall. She wore a bright orange dress and raised her voice as she said, "If they think we're just going to go home without a refund, they're crazy. I paid twenty credits for my ticket."

Another woman said, "Consider yourself luckier than Kate Windsor. She died with her ticket in her hand. Those credits aren't worth your life!"

Dinah rushed toward the woman. "Excuse me, what happened up there?"

The one in the orange dress looked her up and down and then said, "We were lining up in the cloakroom. The woman in front of us swiped her ticket. The screen shouted out her credentials, and then boom, she fell to the floor—dead."

"It must have been a heart attack," the other woman added.

That was all she heard. She kicked her shoes off and charged up the hill. She refused to believe what she had just heard. It could be a mistake. These strangers didn't know Kate. Her friend was young, fit, and strong. She couldn't be dead for no apparent reason. She called Kate's phone, but there was no answer.

A large area in front of the theater had been barricaded. She sneaked into an emergency tent and saw a thin white suit hanging inside. She grabbed the suit and put it on, sliding on a pair of plastic shoes to cover her bare feet. Taking a small medical toolbox with her, she headed toward another section of the secured line.

Two individuals wearing heavy blue suits and large plastic face masks moved in the same direction. She followed closely behind them, matching their stride.

The three moved into the plastic tunnels. She broke off from the two and quickly made her way toward an open tent at the north end. The tent was made of clear plastic walls and was stuffed with people wearing both suits and regular clothes. Computers and other medical gadgets were set up all around the tent. There was a lot of commotion.

The interior of the theater filled with pale yellow smoke. A first grade guard tapped her on the shoulder. "Medical staff aren't allowed," he said.

"But I was called here."

"Detective Tanner said we don't need any medical staff. We need the troops."

"But he called me. Can I just go in and talk to him?"

"No, he left for headquarters."

Dinah waved her arms in the air. "A woman had a heart attack, and medical staff aren't allowed in? What are you talking about?"

The man lowered his voice. "Kate Windsor exploded and killed five others. It's a crime scene."

"Exploded? I didn't hear any explosion."

"It wasn't like a bomb. I wasn't allowed inside, but Detective Tanner said the area was contaminated with some kind of toxic chemical. They're trying to get the people who were exposed but left the theater back to the tent."

"I saw them down the hill. Three women. One in a bright orange dress. She was talking about being in line next to the victims."

"Really?"

There was shouting outside, and the first grade guard to whom she was talking was called on his communicator. "Damn it, more dead people!" he muttered. "Oh, by the way, do you have an ID on you, doc?"

"Huh?"

"May I scan your wrist unit for an ID?" His communicator shouted out again. "Oh, damn it..."

"I told you the three women were heading to the south gate. Go get them before more people die."

He nodded and turned on his heel. As soon as he was out of sight,

Dinah darted over to the transparent wall and peeked inside. She couldn't see into the cloakroom, but she spied a red high-heeled shoe on the floor close to the door. The shoe was unmistakably Kate's. They had each bought a pair while shopping in town together last month. Swallowing a lump in her throat, she shrugged off the white coat and ran out of the tent.

*A*rik walked along the cobblestone path toward his office building at Oxford University. The sun hadn't yet come up, but he was always early for his lecture. It wasn't because he needed to prepare for his class. He had taught this subject for many years, and by now he could give the lecture with his eyes closed. But he loved the tranquility of the campus before sunrise. The early hours in his office were precious to him. A couple of hours later, when students and colleagues arrived, that tranquility would vanish as if it had never existed.

Blues beats and lyrics played in his mind. *Black cat crossed my trail.* He shook his head, trying to brush Rod Stewart's "I Ain't Superstitious" out of his mind, but the song kept playing as if it wasn't in his mind but in the air around him. It was strange. It wasn't even his favorite song.

In the distance, in the dark, he saw a pair of green eyes looking at him. He couldn't see the shape of the animal at all. Just those green eyes. They had to belong to a black cat because its body blended into the darkness. For some unknown reason, he just assumed it was a cat.

He blinked. The eyes blinked. Blinked, and blinked again. Then they vanished.

I need my morning coffee, he thought. He shook his head to brush off the uncomfortable feeling he got from the sound of the songs. Sometimes music triggered painful memories he would rather forget.

"Professor Bonneville," said a squeaky female voice. He almost jumped out of his skin when he heard it. It had come from behind a small bin and some stacked-up tables next to a closed café. From out of the shadows stepped a young female—a student, he assumed—with haunting eyes. Arik shook his head. There was a strange shade in her dark eyes, but like her face, her eyes were youthful.

"Yes," he said. He pulled up the collar of his coat to block the cold breeze nipping the skin behind his neck.

The young student tucked a stray lock of sandy hair under her beanie. "Don't be afraid," she said.

"I beg your pardon?"

"It will pass." She grinned, showing a row of uneven, black front teeth.

"Afraid of what? Who are you?"

"You don't need to know who I am. I have a message for you." She reached her arms forward.

When Arik saw her hands had turned into claws, he jumped backward. His left shoe came down on the slippery, uneven edge of a stone, and he almost toppled over.

"I'm sorry," the girl said again and reached further to pull him in toward her. Fangs appeared in her mouth, and she bit into her bottom lip.

Arik pushed her away from him. A stream of blood ran down from her forehead. He stepped backward again and tripped on another stone. He felt his left ankle twist. "Damn it," he cursed.

"I'm sorry." The girl stopped moving forward. "I'm so sorry, professor!" she cried, her voice no longer squeaky.

"This is a stupid prank!" Arik growled.

A wave of loud laughter came from the back of the building. A male student's voice said, "You've got it, Lucy. You've got him."

Lucy waved her arms frantically. "I'm sorry, professor. I didn't mean for you to get hurt. It was an accident. It was just a dare..." She turned around to run and stumbled over an empty box on the ground. Arik grabbed her elbow just before she fell face first into some trash cans. Her beanie fell, along with a wig, a tube of fake blood, and her fangs.

"Thank you. I'm so sorry..." She twisted out of his grip and scrambled toward the back of the building.

"I know you're from the New Theater group. I'll talk to your professors!" But Arik was speaking to the cold air. The group of students had already disappeared into the darkness, their laughter trickling behind them. Arik wanted to curse. He wanted to call campus security. But what would be the point?

His morning tranquility ruined, he limped toward his office. He wouldn't do any work this morning. Instead, he'd make himself a cup of coffee and read the news on the Internet.

The coffeepot let out a soft whistle when it reached the required temperature. He left his desk and went to his credenza. He poured coffee into a mug, inhaling the aroma of his unique blend, and took his first sip of the day.

Before the rim of the coffee mug touched his lips, a hairy black spider leg reached over the rim from the inside of the mug. He yelped and dropped the mug to the floor. Coffee splattered everywhere. And there was no spider.

"Are you all right?"

He turned around and saw Peter standing at the door.

Arik fixed his tie. "Yes, I'm fine. The mug just slipped out of my hand. You're starting early today, Peter."

Peter smiled. "I have to catch up with marking papers. I promised the students some feedback today. Nice scarf." He pointed to a scarf on the desk.

Arik chuckled. "It's Grace's. I'll give it back to her tonight."

"Oh...someone has a date. That's why you're jumpy!"

Arik said nothing. He grabbed some paper towels from a cabinet and started to clean up the coffee spill.

"You've been going out with her for...what? Over a decade?"

"Five years."

"But who's counting? When are you going to pop the question?"

Arik stood up and glared at his colleague. "Since when did you become so nosy?"

Peter shrugged. "Since when did you lose your sense of humor?"

"You can't lose what you never had. Plus, there's nothing funny about this." He gestured at the mess the coffee had made on the carpet.

"No, you're right. It's not funny at all. Look at your desk!"

"That's a vintage piece of furniture! Not like that veneered desk of yours!"

"The cheap piece of furniture you just referred to isn't mine. I don't decorate my workplace with my own furniture the way you do. There's never a single speck of dust on your desk. Those coffee stains must be driving you insane!"

"I can manage."

"You don't really have a choice. Okay, I'm going to get back to my own business now. Say hi to Grace for me." Peter scurried out of Arik's office.

*D*inah rushed into her office and slammed her palm on the control panel to activate the computer. The computer woke and verified her credentials. She glanced out of the window and saw flakes of white snow starting to fall. Kate loved the snow. Because Iilos controlled the climate and kept it at a perfect level, there was no such thing as snow here. But white snow was Moira's fantasy, a reminder of her homeland. And so they had created something to mimic it.

She shook her head. Would death be artificial, too? When those native to Iilos died, their bodies disintegrated into light particles and were absorbed by an object of their choice. They called it the resting place of an individual's essence. But that wouldn't happen for outsiders like Kate and her.

The computer let out a gentle sound, suggesting it was ready to operate. She turned on the news screen and frowned. There was no breaking news about what had happened at the theater.

She turned on another screen and logged in. She typed in a code and began to surf the police database—another thing that came in handy and Cooper didn't know about was that she was an ass-kicking hacker. She was searching for Detective Tanner, but the system was asking for a passcode. Dinah sighed. It took time to crack codes. She set the machine to run on autopilot and headed to her bedroom.

Her apartment was small enough that it took her only three strides to get to her room. She needed to go back to Xiilok. She wanted to tell Kate's family the news in person. She stuffed her travel pass into her backpack along with a few essential items.

When she opened her closet door, a pair of red high-heeled shoes fell down from the top shelf. She picked them up. Kate detested her masculine boots and fashion sense and always peppered Dinah's clothes collection with as many feminine items as she could.

The evening's events had happened too fast, and Dinah's brain hadn't yet digested the information. Her friend was dead? She refused to believe that until she saw the evidence. A shoe lying on the floor at the theater door could mean anything.

Her computer uttered a happy jingle. She rushed toward it. Access granted! The little hacking program she'd written a while ago actually worked and had performed its magic. Dinah dropped her bag on the floor and dove into the keyboard.

In no time, she was inside the working files folder of Detective Tanner's computer. She flicked through the crime scene photos. Although she'd heard no explosion, the interior of the cloakroom looked like a war zone. Five bodies were on the ground, distorted into unrecognizable shapes by the heat of the fire. It looked as if the bodies had been melted.

And then she saw Kate's black velvet dress, her favorite.

Dinah's tears flowed freely.

Her best friend was really dead.

Kate was like her sister, the only person she knew and trusted in Iilos, and even in the multiverse. The thought of being left by herself in the vast multiverse was terrifying.

After the grief hit her, Dinah felt her blood boil. She understood that she and Kate were outlanders in any universe. They weren't asking for any rights. But Kate's death was undignified. Her body had been mangled and distorted, and her essence had been lost. Her friend deserved better. Lady Iilos had sworn to the multiverse she would make all creatures equal. This was the time. She would ask for her friend's body, regardless of the shape it was in, so it could be properly buried.

It was a crime scene, so they would want to keep the body for investigation. But she would fight. She would get Kate's body back at any cost.

She flicked through pictures. The close-up, graphic photos of the body parts were disturbing. She touched the screen when she saw a close-up photo of the mark below the nape of Kate's neck. She saw the round shape of multiple circles, one inside the other, branded on her skin. It wasn't a meaningless tattoo. It was the mark of a *jumper*— the word they used to describe those who had jumped through the aperture of the multiverse.

Dinah absently touched the mark at the back of her own neck.

She flicked to the next photo.

Very few people in the multiverse knew about this mark. Detective Tanner must have been curious because he had taken several pictures of it.

Wait!

Dinah flicked back to the previous picture. That was Kate's mark. She flicked again to the next one. Although the body was distorted from the explosion, she was damn sure that wasn't Kate's neck she was looking at. She zoomed in on the picture. It was definitely the mark of a jumper.

Another jumper at the same crime scene? It was almost impossible. The odds of having two total strangers who were both jumpers at the same location was as rare as the occurrence of the aperture.

She looked at the time stamp in the corner of the picture. It was the same day but much earlier in the day. She flicked to the next picture and saw another person with the mark, but it had been taken the day before. There were more and more pictures with marks on other individuals, and she wasn't sure now if they were natives to Iilos, space creatures, or outlanders like herself.

She kicked her chair back and rested her face in the palms of her hands. Someone or something was going on a killing spree, exploding jumpers. *Why?*

$\mathcal{M}$adeline nuzzled into the neck of her husband and breathed in the scent of him. She was lying on top of him, so she let her long brunette curls drape over his chest and half of his face. She knew he liked that. But he didn't just lie there and take her commands. He was so incredibly inventive in lovemaking that she would never be able to keep up with his moves. Just like now. He went straight to a point she didn't expect. She yelped then bit lightly at his neck, behind his ear.

"First councillor, we have a meeting and a live broadcast shortly. Can you spare me the embarrassment of appearing in front of six hundred billion citizens with a hickey on my neck?" Ciaran said.

"Keep calling me first councillor and you'll definitely have a hickey."

"First councillor... Ouch!"

Madeline chuckled as her husband began to moan with pleasure. The deep sound coming from his throat always turned her on even more. Out there, he was king of a universe—a warrior and a man who knew it all. But in this room, in this bed, he was her man—the center of her universe. And she knew she was his. With their children, they were at the pinnacle of this family universe. It was something that a year ago, as a journalist in New York, she wouldn't have imagined in her wildest dreams.

The door slid open, and Robert, their home robot, rolled in. Robert had human shape and size and had been designed by Ciaran's father several years ago. He was a learning robot, and his sense of sarcasm had improved greatly by being around Ciaran and herself.

"Obviously, you wheeled in instead of sing the intercom because there's something of urgency on a galactic level that you need to call to our attention to," Madeline said.

"Nothing can justify your intrusion, Robert," Ciaran scolded.

"You have given me permission to intrude if there is a code red message, master!"

Ciaran sat up. "Did you hear that? I bet you learned that from my little brother."

Madeline laughed. Robert had never before called Ciaran "master." But as a learning machine, he learned new vocabulary every day, and he adopted human behavior and rationalization rapidly.

"I learned it from you, unfortunately," Robert said.

"All right, so unlearn it, and I'll install a program that allows you to roll your eyes."

"Thank you. That would be very helpful."

Ciaran threw a robe over his shoulders. "What's the code red message?"

Robert popped open a compartment in the middle section of his body to reveal a folded note.

Ciaran picked up the piece of paper and frowned. "Real paper?"

"Perhaps you can install a program that will allow me to grin. I'm glad you're pleased, Ciaran. Using real paper instead of an electronic notepad has a high probability of creating a sense of nostalgia, which is a positive feeling in humans."

Ciaran smiled. "Nostalgia is only good if your memories are positive. But yes, I'm pleased. Thank you. Is that all?"

"Yes, Ciaran. The message is urgent. I'll leave you to it now."

Robert backed out on his little wheels, and the door of the room slid closed.

Madeline sat on the bed with the blanket wrapped around her body and watched Ciaran as he read the message. When it came to work, he was always focused and intense. She liked watching him work. But taking on the responsibility of king of Eudaiz, a universe far away from Earth, wasn't the task she had wished for him.

The last few months had been very difficult with the pass through the Daimon Gate and his coronation in this strange universe. She would never get used to the number of scars now he bore on that long, lean, muscular body of his. Being king of Eudaiz gave him a special kind of energy—the eudqi. But he hadn't had a chance to adapt to the new energy and utilize it properly.

He wasn't immortal. The eudqi healed almost all injuries, except those where he was hit at the fatal eudqi point on his left shoulder. Madeline frowned at a red scar a few inches away from that point and shuddered.

At that moment, something whizzed past her from behind. Ciaran was looking at her and was about to say something when the object struck him right on his eudqi point.

It was a combat knife.

He hadn't reacted quickly enough. There wasn't time for him to say anything. He looked at her as blood streamed from his wound. The hilt of the knife still vibrated from the impact.

She screamed.

"Madeline!"

She heard Ciaran's voice, calling her name.

"Madeline!"

She felt his arms wrapping around her. She felt every muscle in him quivering.

She opened her eyes groggily. He put her down on the bed and wiped a tear that had fallen onto on her cheek. "You had a psychic episode. You passed out. It must have been bad. I'll get you some water."

She grabbed his hand to stop him from leaving. "No, don't leave."

He sat back down at the bedside. She played with his elegant hands, weaving her fingers in and out of his long ones.

"It was a precognition," she said.

"Anything I should know about?"

"You were stabbed at your eudqi point."

He nodded. "I promise to be careful."

"That's not enough."

"I'll avoid engaging in any situations requiring combat until you feel better."

She nodded. "That's better. Who was the message from?"

"It's from Dex."

She sat up. "Dex?"

"The marshal from the underworld. We were acquainted during my last trip to Earth."

"Oh, *that* Dex. The shapeshifter. What did he want?"

Ciaran sighed. "A package was delivered to one of the underworld jails, and it killed fifty criminals. Dex was called in for an investigation. He found a common and disturbing theme. Twenty out of the fifty deaths were aperture jumpers."

"That's impossible. Didn't we discuss at the council meeting just last week that these apertures have to be identified and closed ASAP? Was it a coincidence that those apertures were on our meeting's agenda?"

Ciaran shook his head. "It wasn't a coincidence. I suggested it. Apertures of the multiverse are loops of light and energy. When people jump through, they absorb that light and energy, and it changes them. Mostly, it enhances their current qualities or talents. But that means that evil creatures, those with dark powers, could become invincible if they jump."

"But you said no person or creature and no system can identify the pattern of their occurrence."

He looked at her, and she could see a deep concern in his striking gray eyes. "One person did."

"Person? You mean a human?"

He nodded and sighed and then waved the piece of paper in his hand. "An old friend of mine identified the aperture pattern once, and he left traces of the results of his work in the system. Now, with this killing frenzy, the multiverse is going to go after him. I have to make a trip to Earth to let him know."

"Why can't you just call him?"

He shook his head. "It's not that simple. Someone has triggered a hunt for jumpers. I don't know the reasons for the killing. But it's not going to stop until whoever triggered it finds what they want. Telling my friend to go into hiding isn't going to solve this problem."

"It doesn't look like I can talk you out of this. So in that case, I'm going with you."

"What? No! You—"

"Stay home with the children?"

"No, I mean—"

"Last time we talked about this and had an argument, you went straight to Babylon and had a fight." She jabbed her finger into his chest. "That scar is a reminder of how close you were to death. And all because of what, Ciaran?"

"Yes, I get the point. I don't have the psychic ability that you have. But that time, there was magic involved. And I don't do magic. This one is pure science. All I need is a computer and some bits and pieces of equipment."

"Are you sure there's no spooky stuff involved this time?"

"Regarding the apertures, yes."

"Regarding things other than the apertures, Ciaran. Things your science can't explain. You said so yourself. You've added so many variables to your scientific equations these days. So much that you are unsure even you can comprehend them. So when your comprehension stops working, you'll need an irrational psychic like me!"

He grabbed her finger that was still jabbing at his chest. "It could be dangerous."

"Aha! You just told me it's only a trip to visit a friend. And now all of a sudden it's dangerous? You're contradicting yourself. And you can't know if there's anything else involved. In short, you'll need me!"

He sighed. "Since when did I start losing ground when we argue?"

She grinned and kissed him.

5

*D*inah grabbed her bag and stuffed whatever she had at hand in it—her laptop, her notepad, her wrist unit, her weapons, and even her paperweight. She shoved everything into the bag so hard trying to zip it up that she ripped the zipper off. She threw the bag angrily, and it flew from one end of the room to the other. Maybe she needed to cry. The grieving in Kate's mother's eyes had been unbearable. But it was better that the news of her daughter's death came from her than from the police. Dinah could only hold on for so long. She really needed to cry.

A tear rolled down her face. She wiped it away.

This was pathetic. She wasn't the crying kind. She'd promised Kate's mother she would find answers. The detective obviously had no clue, or he wouldn't be wasting time taking pictures of the jumper's marks. The pattern was obvious—someone or something was killing jumpers.

The aperture of the multiverse was undetectable. To her knowledge, no one—no creature or computer system in the multiverse—could detect the pattern of its occurrence. That meant the identities of those who had stumbled upon the aperture, like herself and Kate, were virtually unknown. She couldn't imagine the sort of intelligence one would have to possess to be able to identify the jumpers, let alone go around killing them.

Dinah had circled the room so many times, she was making herself dizzy.

Where should she start? She stopped pacing and rushed toward her computer to execute an idea she had just gotten. She placed an anonymous tip about the aperture into Detective Tanner's inbox. Then she carefully erased all traces of the contact in her system and carried on with her research. A short while later, she stared at the computer screen, grinning. She had found an individual who had identified one cycle of the aperture. It was so unprecedented that the name of the person—a human—had been stored in the multiversal database.

It might be nothing. Identifying one cycle could be as random as stumbling upon an aperture. But at least it was a starting point. She had to get to Earth.

She checked her credit account and sighed. She had only enough money for a one-way ticket on the multiversal transport. Figuring maybe she should just get there and figure out the next step later, she ordered the ticket and then finished packing her bag.

She had a license to carry weapons on board, so she took her combat knives and her guns. How to use her weapons on Earth was another matter. But it was better to have them with her than not.

She had been to Earth before on a business trip to Japan, all expenses paid by the client. She had loaded a language program to her system via a computer chip embedded in the language section of her brain. It was still there.

The individual she would pay a visit to this time was Professor Arik Bonneville from England. Her English was good, but she needed to be sure nothing went wrong, so she updated the English language in her system.

She plugged a small chip into her computer that would identify

Arik's precise current location. From experience, she knew England as a location was much too broad.

She pulled her beloved black leather jumpsuit from the closet and put it on. She always felt in top combat form whenever she wore this suit. It wrapped her body like a second skin no matter how many weapons and how much technology she tucked inside it.

She looked into the mirror and flicked her thumb. This was her favorite function. Two gigantic wings spread out from the back of the suit. And it wasn't just for show. She could actually fly with them. It was a tailored design a friend from Xiilok had made for her. She turned around and looked at the wings with pride. She looked like a dark angel with those wings, she thought.

She was about to put her usual chunky boots on when she saw the red high heels. She picked them up. She had to admit she liked the look and the feel of them. They were so feminine. Wondering how she would look in the tight leather jumpsuit and those red high-heeled shoes, she decided to put them on.

She recalled watching a movie called *Catwoman* when she was in Japan. Dressed like this, she thought she looked just like the main character.

The computer beeped an alert. She rushed toward it.

"Oh gosh. No...no. Don't do this to me!" Because she didn't have the money to pay for priority class, she'd had to be on standby and take whatever seat was available in the private express teleport shuttle.

And it was available now.

She collapsed her wings, grabbed her bag, and charged out the door.

She zipped into the private cabin as soon as the robot cleared her. The control board asked for her destination.

"Oh no!" she gasped as she realized she'd left the computer chip with Professor Bonneville's address in her computer at home. There was no time to go back for it now. She punched in a general location in England. The shuttle leaped up in the air and darted into a dark tunnel. The movement was so abrupt, it made her lose her balance and skid toward the corner of the cabin on the polished floor.

Then she realized she was still wearing her red heels.

She rolled her eyes. Red heels and a tight leather jumpsuit... All she needed was the red-light district, and she'd be perfect for a business in Xiilok they called prosexitution, where creatures traded sexual activities for credits.

"Shouldn't you verify the location before zooming into the darkness?" she asked the computer, expecting no answer. Then she saw her typo on the screen. She had typed in "Wingland," and that was apparently where the shuttle was going. She didn't know if it was a real location, but she was sure it wasn't where Arik Bonneville was.

She darted toward the control panel and changed the location. The shuttle swung around suddenly, throwing her onto the floor. She scrambled up to her feet and checked the location again. England was spelled correctly now, but she had to narrow it down. She searched the temporary onboard remote system and located Oxford.

It was better, but it was still a large city. She narrowed it down even further. Each time she changed the destination, the shuttle threw her around like a rag doll. She'd adjusted the route too many times and had run out of credits. The shuttle would throw her out soon. If she had to walk, she wanted to be sure to choose a location as close in proximity to Arik as possible.

She had time to enter something she found in her search that looked like a room number before the shuttle ejected her. As she flew through the air, she promised herself that in the future, even if she had enough money to travel with dignity, she would never use the inter-universal transportation system again.

After hurtling down a short corridor, she crashed into a set of double doors, which burst open on impact. She rolled in not-so-graceful somersaults across the flat floor and then came to a stop.

Crouching on the floor, she watched as one of her red shoes flew into the air, spun around, and landed precariously on a lectern where Professor Bonneville was apparently giving a lecture. She stood up and straightened her back. One of her wings unfurled, pointing straight to the ceiling. She stood on a single high-heeled shoe and looked at Arik.

He was gorgeous. Almost as pretty as a Eudaizian. Not that she had seen a Eudaizian in the flesh nor been to that universe. But she had seen their pictures and heard about their legend. Arik was tall and lean with sandy hair and soft, gentle gray eyes. He looked authoritative as he stood there in a dark suit, his eyes focused on her. The picture she had seen on her computer system didn't do him any justice.

She cleared her throat. "Is this Earth?"

She heard laughter from behind her on the right. She turned around and looked. It seemed that she was in a lecture theater, and at least a hundred students had seen her bumbling entrance.

Arik picked up her shoe from the lectern and approached her. As he closed the distance, her heart skipped a bit. She could smell the masculinity emanating from him. She gave herself a mental slap in the head.

"Yes, I believe it has been Earth for a very long time." He smiled and gave her the shoe. "That was quite a stunt. A much better one than this morning's." He turned toward his students. "The New Theater group has been playing truth or dare all day, and I am, apparently, their chosen victim. Why don't we give…"

"Dinah."

"Why don't we give Dinah a round of applause so that she can go back to her friends and tell them she has met their dare?"

The students clapped.

Dinah bowed as graciously as she could. She had no idea what truth or dare was, but when the audience in the lecture hall applauded, bowing seemed the proper etiquette.

Arik looked at her. "Thank you for the show," he said.

She nodded and turned to leave. Then her right wing felt as if it was going to spontaneously spread. She slapped her left hand to her right shoulder to stop it from opening. As she did so, a needle shot out from beneath her sleeve and punctured Arik's shoulder. His eyes rolled back, and he collapsed to the floor.

The students panicked, and she could see a commotion beginning.

"Don't panic. It's just a sedative. Call for an ambulance. He'll be fine."

6

*T*he hospital's private room was a lot better than the emergency area. When the staff had brought Arik in, followed by Dinah in her outfit that made her stick out like a sore thumb, the emergency area intimidated her. She accidentally knocked over some medical equipment. It shouldn't have gotten in her way, she thought.

Dinah paced the room. Arik looked so peaceful when he was asleep. When she had seen him in the lecture theater, he'd seemed a little tense. She didn't know him at all, so she wasn't sure what it was or what to make of it. But she was sure that on that stage, she wasn't the one who was doing the acting.

A doctor in a white lab coat came in and looked at Arik's chart. He shook his head.

"What's the matter?" she asked the doctor. She had no idea why doctors on Earth were making such a huge fuss about some sedative in her tiny needle.

"You're not his next of kin."

"No. But it's not that serious, is it? He looks as if he's sleeping."

"The sedative in his system is strong enough to knock out an elephant."

"Elephant? Do you mean the large terrestrial animals with large pinnaes and a long proboscis?"

The doctor looked at her as if she had grown a second head. "Yes, but people normally refer to that animal with large ears and a trunk as an elephant."

Dinah ignored his remark. "Can't you just give him an antidote?"

"We can't identify the sedative. We don't have antidotes for drugs we don't even have in our system. I'll call his family in the US. We'll figure out something to help him snap out of this. But I need the permission of his next of kin. How did you find him? How did he end up with that sedative in his system?"

"I found him at the university. I'm from the New Theater group." She grinned, but when the charm didn't warm the doctor any, she continued. "I don't know how he got the sedative. He just collapsed in the lecture hall, and the students called emergency. I followed the ambulance to be sure he was okay."

The doctor shook his head. "Well, he's not." He put the chart back, nodded a goodbye to Dinah, and strode out of the room.

She looked at Arik. "I'm sorry. I didn't know the medical system on Earth was so primitive. I'll fix you. Where I come from, this sedative wouldn't be strong enough to induce even a regular sleep." She shook her head. That wasn't true. The sedative was a street med that she could purchase freely, but she had altered it with her God-given skills in chemistry, turning it into a weapon of sorts.

She glanced outside to ensure no doctors or nurses would be entering the room and then pulled out a needle with the antidote. She searched carefully for a vein on his neck and injected it. "Nice and easy. You'll be fine," she said as she wiped away the drop of blood that appeared on his neck when she pulled the needle out.

In a moment, he began to stir.

She smiled. "You see, I told you you'd be fine." Then she saw he was about to vomit. She jumped out of the way but then thought better of it. She climbed onto the bed and turned him to his side just in time so that he threw up on the floor.

Afterward, she rubbed his back. "Take it easy. It will get better." She climbed over to the other side of the bed and saw that the side of the bed had been dirtied. She pulled out the sheet on the bed to clean things up and accidentally pulled his hospital gown with it.

She had seen naked men before. But this body was the definition of beauty. Long and lean with well-toned muscles. And that...that precious body part was flawless.

She covered him up quickly and looked around for something else to clean up with. Then she spun around to face him again. Maybe she could take one more look at him. There was no harm in looking, was there? She approached the bed, lifted the fabric, and peeked under.

"What are you doing?" said a female voice from the doorway.

Dinah was startled and jumped backward. "Huh?" she said, looking up.

At the door stood a stunning woman with the beauty of a goddess. She was tall and slender with long sandy hair. The woman was so perfect that she didn't seem real. "Who are you?" Dinah asked.

"I'm Grace, Arik's fiancée."

"Oh..." Dinah smiled. "I'm Dinah. I found him at the university. I'm part of the New Theater group. I mean, the students called me. No, I mean, they called the ambulance. He had an accident. But he's fine now."

Arik started to wake, and the system alerted the doctor. The doctor strode into the room, walking past Grace without a glance. He checked Arik's vitals. "How is this possible?" the doctor muttered to himself.

Dinah took small steps backward toward the door, as discreetly as possible so they wouldn't notice her leaving.

"I'm Grace Fontaine, Arik's fiancée," Grace said as she approached the doctor. "Can you tell me his condition?"

"As far as I can tell from the records, you're not his next of kin. But he's no longer critical, so I can give you a report of his condition. The lady here before—" The doctor cut himself off and turned around to look for her. That was all Dinah heard as she charged down the hallway, running outside the hospital.

7

*I*t was cold outside the hospital, and her skintight jumpsuit didn't really help to keep her warm. She checked her wrist unit to see if she had enough credits for a call to Iilos. She knew that every wrong turn she had made while using the inter-universe transport had cost her a lot of credits. But she hadn't planned on it costing almost everything in her account. She had only enough credits to make either a call to Iilos or the job bank.

The short-term solution was to call Cooper and ask him to lend her some credits. The longer term plan was to call the job bank, take a small job, and earn the credits herself. One the one hand, if she called and couldn't reach Cooper, she would be doomed. One the other hand, the job bank wouldn't guarantee her a job, and if she couldn't take what was available, or there wasn't anything appropriate for her, then she would be doomed as well.

Regardless of how charming this little town in Oxford was during the day, as she walked down a small alley, it felt too quiet—and a bit eerie. From the corner of her eye, over a little bridge in a very discreet corner of a small block of cottages, she saw a light flash.

Human eyes wouldn't have caught it, or if they did, it might have looked like a simple camera flash. But Dinah knew what she saw had seen was the most advanced teleport in the multiverse—unlike the dumpster-like public transport she'd been forced to take. And this wouldn't have come from Iilos.

A beautiful couple in their thirties stepped out from that dark corner. What was going on today? It seemed like she kept running into beautiful strangers.

She immediately squeezed herself into a gap between two stone fences and hid. Being small had its advantages. The couple walked right past her hiding place. The woman was tall and lean with big brown eyes and long brunette hair that hung graciously around her shoulders. She wasn't drop-dead gorgeous, but there was something about her that was very compelling. The man, however, *was* drop-dead gorgeous—tall, muscular but slender, striking gray eyes, the face of a dark angel, and thick black hair that almost touched his shoulders.

She could tell by the way he walked that he was her protector. If the universe came raining down on them, he would scoop his woman up and fly her out of harm's way.

"What if Arik doesn't want to cooperate?" the woman asked.

"I'll break his other leg."

Dinah's hair stood up. They were going after Arik! She darted out from her hiding place, behind their backs, raised her arm, and pumped out her sedative needles.

As quick as lightning, as if he had eyes on his back, the man pushed the woman aside, swiveled out of the needles' path, and charged at Dinah. He pulled out two guns.

A two-hand shooter. Hell! She was a two-hand shooter, too, but by the tenacity on his face, she wouldn't stand a chance. She turned, flipped out her wings, and took to the air.

She felt the impact of the laser beams as they hit her wings. If they had been real wings, it would have been painful. But the point was, he had shot at her wings and not her head. One beam on her left wing, and one on her right. Judging by the precision of his shots, he didn't want to kill her.

She dropped down as she was flying over the bridge. She hung onto the concrete rail for several seconds, but before she could let go and jump into the water, the man grabbed one of her hands. She saw a flash on her wrist unit. She knew he had scanned it. In less than a second, he would have seen her Iilos credentials.

She tried to yank her hand away, but his grip was tight. He looked down at her with striking gray eyes. In one swift move, he flipped her over the rail and onto the bridge.

"You're a private investigator from Iilos?" he asked.

She shrugged. "You scanned me, so why bother confirming? Wrist units don't lie."

The man turned and looked at the woman. "She's not a Black Rock or Xiilok creature," the woman said.

"I just need you to say something so that Madeline can judge. Black Rock and Xiilok creatures are notorious for their talent to disguise themselves, and at the moment, they're quite advanced. Wrist units from Iilos can't tell the difference."

"Excuse me! We have the most advanced technology in the cosmos."

He smiled. "We're friends with Iilos. You needn't worry. Why did you attack us?"

Dinah shook her head and said nothing.

"She thinks we're going for Arik and will hurt him," the woman said.

Bloody hell! She had just thought that. The woman was a mind reader. Dinah scowled. "Hey, you don't have permission to peek into my head."

The woman shrugged. "I'm sorry for the intrusion. But without my confirmation, he would have put a beam through your head."

"He would have done it before instead of shooting my wings. I'll take my chances. Stop looking into my mind. I don't like it."

The man smiled. "All right, ladies, don't fight. We don't have forever." He looked at Dinah. "We're Arik's friends."

"So breaking legs is a form of greeting in your universe?" Dinah asked.

Ciaran realized she must have overheard their conversation. "I didn't break his leg, a car did. But that's in the past. We don't mean him any harm. You seem to be protective of Arik. What's your relationship to him?"

Dinah shrugged. She didn't have to answer the question, but she trusted her instincts. This couple seemed to be good people. "I'm not his friend. But I don't mean harm to him. Someone killed my friend in Iilos. I promised her mother I'd find answers. I came across Arik's name during my investigation, and I need his help."

The man's eyes darkened. "You hacked the multiversal database."

She stepped backward. "No, I just found the information in the system."

"That's not possible!" the man growled. He was quite intimidating.

She took another step backward, and one of her heels caught in the uneven cobblestone path. "Ouch!" she said as her ankle twisted. She glanced around over her shoulders. Both of her wings were singed, and now she had only one good leg. She might be in trouble if these two attacked her.

8

*A*rik woke, confused and disoriented. The only things that were clear to him were the eardrum-bursting beats from the heavy metal rock band Sabbath Bloody Sabbath and the fact that he had a pounding headache. Visions of monsters and alien creatures crawling on the bed messed with his head. He knew the images were side effects of the drugs, whatever they were pumping into him at the moment. But the music was loud and all too real.

As he pulled up the sheet to cover his ears, he saw Grace's face hovering over him with a gentle smile. "There you are! How are you feeling?"

"Can you turn that music down?"

She frowned. "What music? There isn't any music. You're in a hospital."

Then he was fully awake. The music vanished, and the quietness returned to the room and to his mind. He glanced around.

"What happened?" he asked.

"I should ask you that question, Arik. We were supposed to have dinner. When you didn't show, I called your cell phone. Your friend, Peter, picked up as the phone was ringing nonstop in your office. He said you were in a lecture and hadn't taken your cell with you. He also said he heard there was an accident there, and he had yet to find out what happened. So I checked with a nurse friend of mine and found you here—with a woman stalking you."

"What are you talking about?"

"There was a woman here. She was from some kind of theater club."

"Oh, Dinah!" He remembered what had happened now. "Yes, she's in a student theater group, and they've been playing truth or dare all day—with me as their target. The last thing I remember was her doing a stunt in the lecture theater. It was quite a spectacular entrance, really. Then something hit me. And I don't remember anything else."

Grace folded her arms. "A spectacular entrance?"

He smiled at her. "Come on, you're not jealous about a student?"

"They're around you like bees with honey. I'm not jealous of your students. If I were, I'd spend my entire life being jealous. But this girl is different."

"You mean her rather interesting choice of outfits? I told you she was putting on a show. And she had a wing, too. It was quite funny."

"I'm telling you, this one isn't an ordinary student."

"All right, the next time I see her, I'll ask if she's really an art student." Then he looked at Grace and sighed. "Okay...I'll make sure there is no next time."

She grinned.

"Can we do dinner again some other time? I'm sorry."

"I need to feed you something. You didn't have dinner, and it looks as if you've thrown up whatever you may have had in your stomach. What do you feel like eating?"

He didn't have an appetite at the moment but figured it might help him to send her for food so he could have some quiet time to himself. He winged it. "A sandwich will do."

"Okay. I'll be back soon," she said and left the room.

He stared at the empty doorway after she'd left, and a feeling of sorrow washed over him. He shook his head. Brooding wasn't going to get him anywhere. It had been five years, and he still hadn't figured out what to do with Grace. She shouldn't have suffered for his sin. People might not describe what she'd been through as suffering, but to him, it was.

He wasn't sure how long he could drag out this relationship. He had a life to live, and five years was a large chunk of it. He left the bed to go to the window, looking down to the street. He felt a prick at the base of his neck. Feeling uneasy, he started to go back to the bed. But then, he saw his ghost.

"Damn you," he muttered. He rushed toward the cabinet and slid into his clothes as quickly as he could. Then he darted outside the room, along the hallway, and down two flights of stairs.

On the street, the man was still standing there. He wore a long black coat and stared at Arik. Five years ago, he hadn't been in a position to negotiate, but now he would make damn sure he took back what was his.

The man turned to walk away. Arik dashed across the street and closed the distance. The man started to run. Arik ran faster.

"Stop!" he called out.

But the man kept running.

When they turned the corner onto a quiet street just past Oxford University, the man suddenly stopped and turned around. He stood in the middle of the road, his hands in the pockets of his long black coat, waiting for Arik. His eyes sparked with an unusual yellow shade.

Arik stopped running and kept his distance.

"It's been a long time, Arik. I have been looking forward to this meeting. As I said when we parted, one day, you will need me."

"I don't need you. I never will. I only want what's mine. I want my life back."

The man chuckled. "You're asking for a lot, Arik. We had a deal. I hope you hold up your end of it."

"There was no deal between us."

"Yes, there was, and you're a man of his word."

"I didn't want to take what you gave me. You can have it back."

The man shook his head. "It doesn't work that way, I'm afraid. You made your decision. I couldn't have imposed anything on you if you hadn't accepted it."

"All right, that was my fault. But Grace didn't have any part in this. Let her out."

"She has you. All her life, this is what she wanted. Why do you think you are in a position to take that away from her?"

"She didn't consent to this!" Arik snarled.

"But she didn't say no, either."

"Bastard." Arik charged at the man. He grabbed at the man's collar, but his hands went right through the man's body. The man vanished and then reappeared behind him.

"The only way you can tell the difference between what's real and what's not is to accept the gift, Arik. Many wanted to take your position—"

"Then give it to them!"

The man shook his head and smiled. "You're very selfish."

"You took advantage of my situation and imposed your stupid gift on me to shackle me for life, and now you call *me* selfish?"

"Well, I would say you took advantage of my compassion for you and made me give you the gift...without knowing you wouldn't even appreciate it. I can't take it back. I have one gift, and it has already been given."

"There has to be a way!"

"Yes, indeed." The man looked straight into Arik's eyes. "You can get rid of my gift when you die. So you either kill yourself, or you wait until you die of old age. But as long as you live, you'll do so with my gift in you. There are many people relying on that gift for salvation. You can live your selfish life for as long as you want—and die with it. Consider it my stupid mistake."

The man nodded a goodbye, turned around, and vanished into thin air, leaving Arik standing alone in the empty street. Then the song by Sabbath Bloody Sabbath began to pound again in his head. He kicked and punched the brick wall until his knuckles tore open. Then he heard Grace's shaky voice.

"Arik!"

The music vanished.

He turned and saw Grace shaking with the cold. He approached her and could see the tears in her eyes. She showed him the sandwich. "I got you some food. And I couldn't find you in the room. I was so scared..." More tears rolled down her face.

He embraced her. "I'm sorry. I won't scare you like that again. You're cold. Let's get you back inside."

In the distance, in the misty air, Arik saw the shadow of the yellow-eyed man again. But he ignored him and took Grace back to the hospital.

9

*D*inah tried her best not to shriek, but her voice still ended up in a high octave. "You're Ciaran LeBlanc, king of Eudaiz!"

"That's right," Ciaran said, glancing at her from the driver seat via the rearview mirror.

"And you're on a mission with your wife, with no guards, and driving a car yourself!"

"This is *not* a car. It's a Koenigsegg exclusive edition. And we are only here without guards because we need to do what we're here for quickly and get out before everyone and his dog in the multiverse figures it out."

Madeline rolled her eyes. "Why don't you just admit you miss your collection of cars terribly and just want to drive because we don't use cars in Eudaiz, Ciaran. We could have done with a less conspicuous vehicle."

"I'll remember that next time, first councillor." He smiled at Madeline, who was sitting in the back seat with Dinah. Dinah knew Madeline wasn't there for company but rather to ensure she couldn't shoot at them from behind.

"If no one knew you were here, how could they deliver your car with just a call?"

Madeline smiled. "He has a very extensive business set up here, and the system is always in place for him. But then again, the last time he used it, someone interfered with the signal. It might be more secure now, but we still need to be very careful."

"And you promised me a call to my friend in Iilos when we get to your place. We can use a more generic system, right?"

"Absolutely," Ciaran said.

"Look out!" Madeline shouted and pointed ahead.

"What?"

"A man on the road!" Dinah yelled.

Ciaran was traveling at an incredible speed. He slowed down but didn't slam on the brakes. "I don't see a man."

They felt an impact as if the car was being pushed to the side. Ciaran floored the brake and fishtailed. As soon as the car stopped, he bolted out of the car. Madeline jumped out from the back seat.

"Oh hell!" Dinah muttered and slid out, putting her weight on her one good leg.

"Behind you!" Madeline shouted.

Ciaran swung a back kick and felt the impact, but he still couldn't see the person. As soon as the man fell on the ground and rolled away from Ciaran, Madeline charged and attacked him. But he was a lot stronger than she was. After a few rounds of exchanging blows, he kicked her and sent her rolling backward.

Ciaran prowled angrily. Judging from the direction of Madeline's defense, he joined in for some wild hits—and misses.

"Her left, and behind!" Dinah shouted.

Ciaran pulled his gun and shot in that direction.

"He's been hit," Madeline said and rolled away. But as soon as she did so, she was no longer an anchor for Dinah's directions.

"Coming from your right!" she shouted.

Ciaran fired but missed.

"Knife at front!" Madeline shouted.

Ciaran jumped backward, shooting in front of him at the same time. But the man swiveled aside, and his knife slashed at Ciaran's side.

"Your back!" Dinah shouted in anticipation.

Ciaran swung a back kick as he couldn't change direction fast enough when she shouted out his move. He hit the man in his path. The man fell, rolling on the ground. Then he crouched and looked at Dinah

"Oh hell! He's going to charge at her," said Madeline.

Dinah limped backward.

Seeing the movement, Madeline darted at the man, but he kicked her away with ease.

As fast as lightning, Ciaran darted past the man he couldn't see and scooped Dinah up, carrying her in one arm as if she were a doll.

"Turn left!" Dinah shouted. Ciaran turned to his left, facing the man. She pointed her right arm and shot a needle from the sleeve of her suit.

She hit the man between the eyes. He staggered and slumped to the ground. His body glowed, and Ciaran could see him now. He lowered Dinah to the ground and approached him. Crouching next to the dying man, he asked, "Who sent you?"

The man looked at Ciaran, his eyes shining in a reddish shade. Grinning, he said, "The leader of the Xiilok rebels sends you his regards, Ciaran LeBlanc."

Then his body exploded into a whorl of red fumes, which enveloped Ciaran. Ciaran felt to the ground.

"Fucking robot bomb," he muttered. He lay down, gasped for air, and then passed out.

Madeline rushed toward him. "Don't! Stay away!" Dinah shouted at Madeline. "Stay away, Madeline. They're toxic fumes designed to kill Eudaizians."

"You want me to let him die?" Madeline paced the ground.

"There's nothing you can do. Leave him to me," Dinah said and limped toward Ciaran. She flipped open a pocket on her left sleeve. If it was toxic fumes, she had an antidote for it. She pulled out a needle and sighed. This was her top-range needle, and she had only one.

She hoped no one else got hurt before she could get back to Iilos and make more.

She turned Ciaran's neck slightly, found a vein, and jabbed in the needle. "Come on, breathe for me," she said. She placed her palms on his chest and pressed. One. And two. And three. Then he gasped and resumed breathing.

"He's okay now."

Madeline approached. "We have to get out of here before more of them come."

They put him in the back of the car. Madeline got into the driver's seat and stared at the complicated dashboard. She shook her head, squared her shoulders, and turned on the engine.

The car roared and stormed forward. Madeline was going too fast, and the pedal seemed too sensitive for her to operate manually. She took her foot off the accelerator. The car stopped instantly. Dinah was thrown to the floor of the car. She braced herself against Ciaran's body to stop him from rolling to the floor as well.

"This isn't going to work," Madeline muttered.

"You have the address?" Dinah asked.

"I believe it would be installed in my wrist unit."

"Scan it to the operator panel."

Madeline followed her instructions. The car hummed slightly, and a soothing female voice came out of the speakers. "Have a safe journey."

Then the car rolled away, driving itself.

Madeline waved her arms. "I should have guessed. He wouldn't drive a lesser car!"

10

*C*ooper glanced around to be sure the long hallway in front of Dinah's apartment was quiet. He didn't want to surprise the neighbors. She hadn't come to the office as she had promised. And she hadn't responded to any of his messages. Calls to her went to the oblivion. It was very unlike her. Then he heard about the incident at the theater. After scrambling through security of a galactic scale, he knew she wasn't among the dead. But Kate was.

He knew Kate, and goddammit, he liked her. He got a small electronic pin and quickly jabbed at the lock. His device never failed him. Dinah would hate this, but the situation called for it, so he broke into her apartment.

The small apartment wasn't as he remembered it. It was like a war zone—as if Dinah had left in a hurry. *She didn't even leave me a message*, he thought. He made his way to the blinking computer. He activated the computer, but when it asked for a passcode, he gave up.

Cooper was a street-smart kind of guy. Technology wasn't his friend.

While he was looking at her journal on the desk, he noticed a chip in the computer. Her computer would ask for a passcode, but the chip wouldn't. He smiled and pulled it out. As he tilted his head to grab the chip, a laser beam shot past him and hit a picture on the wall behind him. It exploded and fell to the floor in pieces.

He pulled the chip out and lay flat on the ground. He heard someone push the door open and walk into the apartment. The person approached his position on the floor, and Cooper stayed as still as he could. He could see military grade boots, and he recognized the steps of a combat-trained individual.

Your training is about to be wasted, he thought and pointed his gun. He fired. His beam traveled upward from the lower abdomen and through the body. It exited at the top of the man's head and hit the ceiling above. But instead of seeing the splatter of blood, he heard a muffled sound as if he had hit a sandbag.

"Damn you, robot," he cursed and sat up as the body of the robotic assassin melted down into a metallic pool on the floor.

"Dinah will really hate you when she sees the stains you're making on her carpet. What a waste!" he muttered and stood up. He nudged the computer chip into his pocket and headed back to his apartment, where he knew his computer wouldn't shout at him for a passcode.

After plugging in the chip, his computer revealed the data. Dinah's search journal was in a text file. She had tipped off Detective Tanner about a possible outbreak of attacks on people who had been through the apertures. Cooper leaned back in his chair. The apertures of the multiverse were not at all common knowledge. He knew of them but had never had an encounter with people who had been through them, nor had he handled any cases related to them.

Dinah had searched for locations—Oxford, England. Professor Arik Bonneville? *What the heck is this about?* he wondered. But at least he could deduce Dinah's current whereabouts from this data. It explained why his call to her wouldn't go through. Inter-universal calls cost an arm and a leg. He'd have had to agree to terms, conditions, and, of course, payment before anything would connect.

He sighed. If he could get to her and then take the Xiilok job, that would pay for the expenses. He was worried about her. That was the main reason he had tried to call her. Credits were just currency. He spent them, and he'd earn them back. But a friend like Dinah was hard to come by.

He looked at the description of the contract from Xiilok. He understood the delivery part. But the chemical compound assembly process was gibberish to him. Maybe he should just forget about it. Dinah had enough on her shoulders. He'd just called to make sure she was okay.

He connected and waited for the signals. After jumping through hoops, he finally got the ringtone of her wrist unit, but the sound coming out from it made his blood run cold. It was a humming sound in waves, a deep sequence in a language he didn't recognize. It was the sound of space creatures.

11

*A*rik headed back to his office to get his cell phone. It was late. He frowned at the light pouring out of the windows of the hallway leading to his office. *Who'd be working at this hour?* he thought.

He adjusted his scarf, pulled off his gloves, and pushed open the heavy oak door that led to the ground floor level.

From the stairs at the end of the corridor, he could see light emanating from his office. He walked along the corridor, trying not to make any noise. His office door was open slightly. From inside, he could hear a bluesy guitar and Eric Clapton singing "Crossroads."

"I went down to the crossroads, fell down on my knees."

"That's enough, you bastard," Arik snarled and kicked the door open. In front of him was a quiet office, neat and tidy as it always was. The coffee stains had been cleaned up. Grace's scarf was still on the desk where he'd left it.

It was as quiet as any other night. So quiet he could hear himself breathing.

He checked his desk drawer. His cell phone was still there, waiting for him. He turned on the phone and checked the last call. It was from Grace, as she had said. There was another call from his mother. He sighed. The doctor had mentioned they had contacted his family in the US when they thought he wouldn't snap out of the sedative's effects. He called his mother. She picked up immediately. It was like she'd been waiting.

"How are you, Arik?"

He could feel the pain in his mother's voice, and he was sorry to have caused that. He hadn't talked to her for months, and then the first thing she heard after all that time was the doctor's call.

"I'm sorry, Mother. It was a misunderstanding. I should have called you earlier."

"Don't worry, Grace called and said you were fine. She's a good woman, Arik."

"Yes, Mother. I've never said any different."

"You've been going out with her for a long time..."

"Mother!"

"All right, I won't mention that again."

"How is everyone?"

"We're all fine. Why don't you call and ask them yourself?"

"I talk to Jenny all the time."

"You mean you Facebook her."

"It's a form of communication, Mother. It's efficient."

"All right. I'm glad you're fine. But you have to do something about your students. They shouldn't be playing truth or dare and causing accidents. There has to be discipline. It's Oxford University after all, isn't it?"

"Is that what Grace told you?"

"Isn't that what happened?"

He chuckled. "Yes, it is. Students are young, Mother."

His mother laughed. It was good to hear her laughter. "Yes, you did much worse when you were their age. Remember the van you had when you toured around with your band?"

"Please don't bring that up."

"No, no, it was very funny. Someone bought that bomb of a car you had and drove it past our house. Jenny recognized it. Didn't she tell you—or Facebook you?"

"People buy old cars all the time. It's really not that big a deal."

"Your time here is a joy in my memories, Arik. That's all I have left of you now."

"Don't say that, Mother."

"Okay, you're about to say you've got to go, so I'd better wrap up. There are a few letters here for you and a package. Do you want me to send them over?"

"Who's the package from?"

"I don't know. I don't recall seeing the sender's name. Let me check—"

"Don't worry, Mother. I may take a vacation soon. I'll visit and take care of the mail."

"Really? When?"

"Soon. In a couple of weeks if it's okay with you."

"Oh Arik, do you need to ask? Anytime, son. Anytime. Do you want me to tell your father?"

"That's up to you."

"All right, you've got to go."

He chuckled. "Yes, it's quite late here."

"Goodbye, Arik."

He held on to the phone for a short moment and then disconnected.

"Are you okay, Arik?"

He jumped out of his skin and cursed at Peter, who was standing at the door.

"Goddammit," he muttered. He heard "Crossroads" playing again.

"What? You don't like the song? It's my favorite," said Peter.

"What?"

"Arik, I thought you were cultured. You played in a band when you were young, didn't you? What do you listen to these days? Dido?"

"So you've been listening to those blues songs all day long?"

"Yes. I hate grading papers. The legendary songs keep my spirits up."

Arik shook his head, flopped down in his chair, and laughed. He wasn't going insane after all. "No, it's all good, Peter. And thanks for picking up the phone when Grace called."

"No problem. What's with the accident?"

Arik shrugged. "It was nothing. Students playing truth or dare."

"Really? What students?"

"The New Theater group."

"Nah, can't be."

"Why's that?"

"They broke up last year and didn't renew this year."

Arik nodded.

Peter raised his mug of tea as a goodbye and walked away.

12

*D*inah could feel the flesh on her backside melting. She had sat in the same spot for far too long. She looked down the long marble corridor of the mansion and wanted to pace, but her ankle was swollen to the size of a small orange, so she forced herself to abandon the urge. She had lost her wrist unit during the commission in town. So at the moment, she had absolutely nothing. No credits, no identification, and no way to call Cooper. The door at the end of the grand hallway slid open, and Ciaran and Madeline stepped out. Ciaran had regained his kingly aura and was as magnificent as always. *Madeline must be pleased,* she thought.

"Thank you for helping out before, Dinah," Ciaran said. "I apologize for having doubted you. You mentioned you wanted to call Iilos?"

She shrugged. "I've lost my wrist unit. It's not like I can just call a number. Without identification, no calls from me will go through. At least, that's the system in Iilos."

Madeline smiled and said nothing.

Ciaran said, "It's the same in Eudaiz. And can you guess who designs and is in charge of the system there?"

"You. But Iilos and Eudaiz are two different universes. Unless you can hack..."

Ciaran stood and merely smiled.

"Oh my god, so you *do* hack systems!"

"It's my favorite mental exercise. But first, let me fix this ankle."

"Oh...really? Are you sure?"

Ciaran smiled and crouched in front of her. "When I was on Earth, I fixed a pig's tail before. The pig survived." He took her shoe off. "Relax."

Madeline chuckled. "The pig survived. But he didn't guarantee its tail was okay."

"What?"

She heard a crack as Ciaran straightened her crooked ankle. "This should be better than the pig's tail." He smiled and held up a small pill. "I know you're a walking talking chemical weapons and medicine cabinet, but this little pill will reduce the swelling very effectively."

She took the pill and grunted out a thank you. She didn't like being handled.

"Now we'll get you to the computer room, where I'll arrange a call for you. We also need to do some research there. And before I forget, I am interested in a sample of your weaponry clothing."

"Are you trying to talk me out of my clothes?"

Ciaran laughed.

"I think she'd be very happy to take them off for you," Madeline said and grinned.

"Hey! I told you not to peek into my mind!"

Madeline shrugged. "I'm protective of my man."

Ciaran smiled. "You have considerable skills, Dinah. I'll bet you know chemicals, computer programming, and hacking. And this weapon suit of yours is very effective. I can guarantee you a very attractive position in Eudaiz if you're so inclined."

Oh my god, a job offer Cooper would kill for! She cleared her throat. "I'll think about it. But I'm very happy where I am at the moment."

Ciaran nodded. "As you wish." Then he scooped her up in his arms again and carried her with him to the computer room.

"I'm also interested in how you know that the chemical used on me was specifically targeted for Eudaizians," he said as he walked.

"Sure, I can tell you."

"Also, the formula of your antidote—"

"You're asking for a lot, Ciaran."

"Well, we make really generous offers to recruit talent."

"I'll wait until I see your offer."

He smiled.

Calling what they had entered a computer room was an understatement. This was an arsenal of computers and related equipment that looked as if it could control a galactic war. If this was only a small station Ciaran had put on Earth, she couldn't imagine what it would be like in Eudaiz. She could only dream of having this amount of resources to work with. She liked her job offer already, whatever it might be.

It took Ciaran precisely three seconds to hack her system in Iilos and put her call through to Cooper. Only three seconds to insult the system she had worked for a lifetime to earn enough credits to buy.

She called four times and couldn't get a response from Cooper, so she gave up. But her concern was eating her up, and it grew worse by the second. *Where is Cooper?*

"Dinah?" Ciaran called out.

"Huh?"

"Which port did you use to search for Arik's information?" He pointed at the monitor.

Her jaw dropped. He was inside her computer in Iilos and was hacking the police system from her computer. And he did this for *sport*. So much for multiversal data security! Or maybe he was truly a freak show.

"I can find out, but it will be much more efficient for you to tell me. Plus, I don't want to stumble upon any information in your computer you don't want me to see. I can see you hacked into the police database and Detective Tanner's files. But I'm only interested in Arik and the multiversal apertures."

"Fifty. Port fifty."

He nodded. "Thank you." Ciaran kept searching. His fingers flew across the keyboard. Then he stopped, stared at the monitor, and pushed his chair back. He looked at Dinah.

"What? I do that all the time. I sneak in for a bit of information to do my job. I didn't misuse the information."

He shook his head. "The system isn't vulnerable."

"It's not good news, Ciaran?" Madeline asked.

He shook his head. "Dinah could see the information because someone *let* her see it."

"Should I take that as an insult?" Dinah asked.

Ciaran sighed. "That part of the databank is incorruptible. Someone who has access to the system has Arik's information and has been feeding it to others. You are not the only one who got the information. Every lead points toward the fact that Arik might have found the pattern of the apertures."

"Why? What can someone get to make the multiverse hunt for Arik?" Madeline asked.

"It might be a red herring," Dinah said.

Ciaran nodded. "There must be an incentive for killing jumpers."

"I'm a jumper."

"I beg your pardon?"

"I'm a jumper myself." She showed the mark below the nape of her neck. "I did that when I was like five. Kate and I were playing in the field outside our village. Then we saw something, like a rainbow. So we jumped without knowing what it was or what we were doing. I just found out a few years ago and told Kate. But the jump didn't change us or make us any different. At least, in my case. I certainly didn't grow any taller!"

"Are you sure?" Ciaran asked.

"My kills are trained. I don't see any enhanced natural talent in my case. So killing jumpers like me isn't going to benefit anyone."

"What about Kate?" Madeline asked.

"She was even more normal than me. Strong, healthy, beautiful, and smart. She always was. And I've known her my whole life."

"How did it happen, may I ask?" Ciaran said.

"We were supposed to have a girls' night out. When I got to the theater, it had already happened. People said Kate fell as if she'd had a heart attack—and then she died." She drew in a breath. "Judging by the photos of her body, the chemical was strong, nasty, and airborne. I don't think anyone in Iilos could get their hands on a chemical with that kind of potency."

"The package from the underworld had a Eudaizian tag on it," Ciaran said.

"Really? It was sent from Eudaiz?" Dinah asked.

Ciaran shook his head. "No, it's a fake tag. Carrying a Eudaizian tag would easily get the package past a lot of quarantine systems. But only an insider or someone who used to be an insider would be able to fake that."

Madeline waved her arms in frustration. "No. If you're thinking about him, it's not possible, Ciaran. He died. I couldn't sense a whiff of him here or in the multiverse."

"Who?" Dinah asked.

"The worst kind, Dinah," Ciaran said. Then he looked at Madeline. "I could think of one reason why someone would want to do this —to create chaos. Everyone wants to hunt Arik down because they think he knows when the next aperture will be. Jumpers will fear for their lives. Ordinary people will fear more attacks. And this fear will snowball. And then? Chaos. And who would benefit from that if not Hoyt, Madeline?"

Madeline shook her head. "He's dead."

"Why don't we just go tell Arik. Wouldn't that be the first sensible step?" asked Dinah.

Ciaran nodded and stood up. "It's a sensible step if he's sensible enough to listen."

"Why wouldn't he?" Dinah asked.

Ciaran shook his head. "You'll see."

13

The trendy bar was crowded with people enjoying pre-dinner drinks. Ciaran looked at his wrist unit to confirm the address. "He's here," Ciaran said to Madeline on his right and Dinah on his left. Dinah was still limping, but the swelling had gone down considerably.

They crossed the front of the bar to a less crowded area that seemed to serve as the dining area. A group of young people on a hen night rushed past, pushing everyone aside. They laughed and rushed away.

A girl from the group was left behind, clumsily picking up the hem of her long dress and struggling across the polished floor on her ridiculously high heels. She tripped on her dress and fell forward into a tall shelf full of glasses and bottles. The shelf toppled and was going to fall on top of Dinah. She knew she couldn't get out quickly enough with her sore ankle. As he had done before, Ciaran scooped her up in his arms and swiveled away from the crash.

He stumbled over a small drink cart and stopped suddenly. Dinah's legs swung with the momentum. One of her shoes slipped off and flew through the air, landing gently on a table where she could now see Arik and Grace about to have dinner.

Arik and Grace looked at Ciaran standing there with Dinah in his arms.

Arik stood, picked up the shoe, and approached them. He slid the shoe onto Dinah's foot. "It's a pleasure to see you again, Dinah. I can see you now have a partner for your show."

Arik and Ciaran locked eyes with each other. Ciaran put Dinah down and reached his hand out for a handshake. "Good to see you, Arik. You look well."

Arik cast a glance at Ciaran then turned on his heel. He went back to the table, grabbed his coat, and escorted Grace out of the restaurant.

Ciaran turned and followed him outside. Madeline and Dinah followed. Across the street, they caught up with the couple. "We need to talk, Arik."

Arik ignored Ciaran and kept walking.

Madeline stepped forward. "Arik, I don't know what happened between you two, but it's important that we talk. People's lives—and your life—are at stake."

Arik turned around. "Thank you for your concern, but what happened between us is none of your business."

"You've just addressed my wife. What happens to me *is* her business," Ciaran snarled.

"Your wife? Which one?"

Madeline smiled. "If you want to bring Juliette into the conversation to cause friction between us, then you are mistaken, Arik. She was his wife. His past. I know her, and I accept the fact that he had a life before me. Any more remarks?"

Ciaran approached and wrapped his arms around Madeline's shoulders. "It's not worth it, Madeline. Let's go. Let him die."

Madeline didn't turn away with Ciaran. Arik approached, looking her up and down. "What's your name?"

"Madeline."

"Madeline, I guess you know we were like brothers until my girlfriend fell for his pretty face and married him. Which was fine. She was a free woman. But she didn't last long inside that secret house of his. When she died, I was banned from her funeral."

"I didn't stop you from coming!" Ciaran snarled.

Arik flipped his shirt up, revealing a long scar above his waist. "You hoped I died in that dark alley like a dog, didn't you?"

"I didn't do this!" Ciaran was obviously upset. He looked at Madeline. "I didn't know anything about this," he said.

"Oh, so you didn't know your family was a bunch of corrupt mafia members?" Arik said.

Ciaran punched Arik in the face. "Don't you ever accuse my family of anything. I said I didn't do it. That means *no one* in my family did it."

"You don't know jack about your people, so don't guarantee their actions!"

"If people betray me, they are no longer my people. So I'll say it again, no one in my family hurt you."

"You think I brought this on myself?"

"You weren't exactly innocent, Arik. Juliette didn't leave you for me. She wanted to save herself!"

Arik punched Ciaran. The two men lunged at each other and traded blows. Madeline grabbed Ciaran, and Grace grabbed Arik, pulling them apart.

Grace asked, "When was this?"

"A lifetime ago," Ciaran snarled.

"When?" Grace asked Arik.

"Six years. About that time," Arik said as softly as he could.

Grace stepped backward. "Why can't I remember any of this?" Tears rolled down her face. She walked away.

Arik rushed after her. "It was before your time with me."

"I don't believe you..." She looked at him then moved away again. "I have no memories at all. It's not possible."

"Someone has a skeleton in the closet. It should be a good one to be worth the fuss," Ciaran said.

Arik growled and wanted to attack Ciaran again, but he thought better of it and followed Grace. She whirled around and snapped, "Don't follow me."

He recoiled. "I can explain."

"No. And even if you could, it shouldn't have taken six years." Then she walked away.

Arik turned and looked at Ciaran. "There's a brick wall across the road." He pointed. "I'm not going to be your punching bag."

"All right, now you two can talk like two civilized adults," Madeline said and turned to leave.

"Someone didn't exactly clean all of his *own* skeletons out of the closet!" Arik said.

Ciaran turned and was about to respond to Arik. But then he thought better of it and followed Madeline.

"Madeline!" Ciaran called out.

"If you need to fight, feel free to do so. I'm not getting in between you two. Remember, you're no longer in your twenties. Don't make fools of yourselves." She pointed at Dinah. "I am going to take this lady shopping. She needs some better clothes."

"Madeline..." Ciaran tugged at her elbow.

"Do you need clothes, too, Ciaran?"

"No." He released her arm. "Please be careful?"

Her eyes softened. "All right. You too."

14

*T*he waitress approached with a gracious smile on her face. "What can I get you?" she asked as she put the menus on the table.

Dinah sat opposite Madeline in a small booth at the café. She grabbed a menu and glanced at it. She shouldn't eat any Earth food without knowing the exact ingredients and the effects the food combinations would cause. She still regretted eating the sushi with raw fish on her trip to Japan.

"Do you have ice cream other than this?" Madeline asked, pointing at an item on the dessert list.

The waitress frowned. "That's the rainbow ice cream. It has seven flavors."

"It's freezing outside, Madeline," Dinah said.

"Okay, get me a tub of each flavor."

"Do you mean a scoop of each?"

"I mean a tub!" Madeline said.

"All right then. And you, ma'am?"

"I'll share with her...if you don't mind, Madeline?"

Madeline shrugged. The waitress scurried away.

Dinah leaned back in her chair. "I'm offended, Madeline."

"Why? Because I offered to buy you new clothes?"

"Well, I offered to take my clothes off for your drop-dead gorgeous husband, and you didn't even blink. But now the fumes of jealousy are oozing out of every pore on your body, eating you up and making you want to swallow an entire universe of iced sugar. And simply because someone mentioned the name of your husband's ex. Of course, I feel offended!"

"I'm not jealous."

Dinah snorted. "So you didn't know Ciaran had to fight for Juliette and ditch his best friend for her, right?"

"You don't know what we've been through regarding Juliette. Don't even try to guess."

"So tell me."

The ice cream was delivered, and the tubs took up the entire table.

Dinah picked up a spoon and dipped it into a tub containing pink ice cream. "It looked like you didn't know as much as you thought you did," she said.

Madeline shook her head. "I'm on this mission because of my psychic ability. But I can't read Arik's mind. There are very few people I can't read. But Ciaran didn't know I couldn't read his mind. Did you see the look on his face when Arik mentioned a fact he didn't know about? That's the fear of uncertainty. He didn't know how much more Arik knew. And that I could read all of the information he didn't want me to know. Ciaran is always in control of his information. But at that time, he wasn't, and he didn't like it at all."

"Nah, I didn't see it that way. I didn't know the back-story, but on the surface, all he cared about was your conclusion at this very moment. He can't control your thinking, especially when it's clouded with jealousy."

"I'm not jealous!"

"How did she die?"

Madeline shook her head as if she didn't want to talk about it.

"You can't compete with a dead woman. The way he thinks of her is locked in his mind and his memories. You can't change that. And I could have guessed Ciaran was one of the few people whose mind you can't read. Otherwise, you wouldn't be sitting here pondering."

"Damn it, Dinah."

"I'm an investigator."

"You'd have to be before I pay attention to any of your conclusions."

"I'm not a good investigator. I'm an excellent one. What did you do before you met Ciaran? Were you a journalist?"

"What makes you say that?"

She shrugged. "Just the way you think. Journalists report facts, make deductions from the information, put their spin on things, and then re-communicate. In a nutshell, they interpret facts. On the contrary, investigators tell the difference between fact and opinion. Skilled investigators don't draw conclusions because the minute they do, they insert their own opinion into things. And opinion equals subjectivity. Investigation 101." Dinah shoved her spoon into a yellow tub. "This is good," she muttered.

Tears gleamed in Madeline's eyes.

Dinah spooned out some blue ice cream.

Madeline said, "She died for him. Twice. Before we even got involved, Ciaran told me the love they had for each other in their twenties was irreplaceable. I accepted that. When Ciaran said if people betray him, they're no longer his people, he meant it. He doesn't forgive and forget. But he did for her." A tear rolled down her face.

Dinah reached for a tub full icy green sweetness.

"She loved him, used him, betrayed him, then died for him. But he forgave her even before she died. And during that time, I wasn't there." Another tear rolled down her face.

"You weren't there because you didn't know him yet?"

"I was married to him at that time. I wasn't there because we'd had an argument the day before, and we parted. We were in a battle before his coronation." Then came another tear.

Dinah nodded. "I agree. You're not jealous. What happened on the street just now hit a sore spot. And—this is my opinion as a fellow woman—that sore spot isn't going to go away. There's nothing you can do about it."

"I know!" Madeline wiped her tears.

"But you have two trump cards. One, his love for you is enormous. I can see that with my own eyes. And two, you're alive." She pushed the tub of vanilla ice cream toward Madeline. "Now eat this before I finish it all."

After a while, they went back to the spot where they'd left the men. Ciaran and Arik sat on the sidewalk, leaning against the wall, with a few bottles next to them. They stood up as Madeline and Dinah approached. Dinah could see a few more bruises on both men's faces. They had apparently gone through a few more rounds of scuffling before finding peace in alcohol. *Is it only human men who are weird, or is that a multiversal issue?* she thought.

"How is this outfit," Ciaran gestured up and down at Dinah, "better than the one she had on before?"

Dinah wore chunky boots, strategically tattered jeans, and a leather jacket.

"I agree," Arik said in a slurred voice.

"Oh my god, are you both drunk?" Madeline asked.

Ciaran grinned and said to Arik, "My wife doesn't think I can handle a few drinks for old time's sake."

Dinah could feel the contents of her stomach welling up. Ciaran saw her reaction and jumped out of the way just as a stream of half-digested ice cream hit Arik's pants and shoes.

"Xiilok creature!" Madeline said.

"Where?" Ciaran whirled around, moving Madeline behind him. She pushed him aside easily and darted toward a small bridge where they now saw a man with yellow eyes standing. Ciaran charged after Madeline.

Arik asked Dinah, "Are you okay?"

"No, but I'm sober," she said and ran after Madeline and Ciaran. Arik followed her. When she got to the bridge, Madeline, Ciaran, and the man with yellow eyes were nowhere to be found.

"Ciaran said Madeline is psychic. She can track minds. What's your talent?" asked Arik.

"Well, I'm not psychic."

Dinah glared at him as he hiccupped.

15

*I*n a small alley a long distance from the bridge, the yellow-eyed man stopped running and turned around. "You're fast, Eudaizians."

"This one is high-ranked, Ciaran," Madeline said between her teeth to Ciaran. "I don't sense hostility in him."

Ciaran nodded.

"We can do a lot more damage to you than running. Who are you, and what do you want?" Ciaran asked.

"I am your friend."

Ciaran smiled. "And we are not your friends. But your friendly intention is noted. Now tell us what you want, and keep your distance."

The man nodded. "I understand why you're being cautious. I'm a Xiilok rebel."

Madeline and Ciaran pulled their guns at the same time. Seeing the intensity of the situation, the man stepped back.

"You sent a Xiilok robot bomb to kill us. So much for your friendly intentions," Madeline said. She felt strange and a bit dizzy.

But still, she didn't sense this man was a killer. *Stay focused*, she told herself. *Ciaran needs you.*

The man raised his hand to show he had no weapons and didn't mean any harm. "Please, hear me out. I never agreed to harm Eudaizians. There are two major camps of rebels in Xiilok. But no matter whether we're from the red or yellow camp, we can't afford robot bombs. We don't even have guns. We don't benefit at all from killing you."

"Did you send packages to kill the aperture jumpers?" Ciaran asked.

The man hesitated.

"Lying to us isn't going to do you any good," Ciaran snarled.

"I disagreed with them! Violence doesn't help the situation."

"Well, your opinion didn't save those your camp killed."

"No, it didn't. That's why I need your help. Arik has a gift I gave him. You have to make him use it."

"Why don't you tell him yourself?"

"I tried."

The world in front of Madeline become blurrier by the second. The next thing she knew, she fell into Ciaran's arms.

"What did you do?" Ciaran shouted at the man.

"I didn't do anything."

"Madeline, darling, tell me what's happening!"

She opened her mouth to say something, but no words came out. She tried again. "Can't breathe." She gasped for more air.

"Okay, sit down here. Calm down and try taking deep breaths for me." She tried. She could feel his hands holding her, but she couldn't see much. *Focus. He needs me.* She willed all of the Eudaizian power in her, concentrated, and tried to breathe. She thought about her children, about the battles they had been through. She had a beautiful family now. She had to live to cherish it. A burst of fresh and cold air came into her lungs, but she knew it wouldn't last long.

She opened her eyes and saw Ciaran's face close to hers. "Try to hang in there. I'll take you back to Eudaiz right now. I'll open the teleport."

"Was she exposed to the robot bomb?" the yellow-eyed man said.

Ciaran turned and looked at the man. Madeline could see the man standing right behind Ciaran, looking down at her. If he meant to cut Ciaran's throat, it would have happened by now. When she was down, he was totally defenseless.

"I was, directly," he said. "How far can it spread?"

"I don't know. But I do know it's airborne. You can't take her back to Eudaiz. If she was exposed and infected, she'll become another bomb herself. Check to see if there's a red dot on her arm."

Ciaran pulled her left sleeve up and found nothing. He pulled up her right sleeve. And there it was, a glaring red dot.

"Would he be infected again, being around me?" she asked.

"No. If he somehow survived it, he's immune."

"How long does she have?" Ciaran asked.

"I don't know."

"Have you seen this poison before?"

"No. We don't have the skills to either make it or create an antidote. I just know about it. There's a group in Xiilok who specialize in this. But they're commercial. They're not part of the rebels. The antidote is what you need now. Do you want me to ask that group? If you have the money to pay, they'll do anything for you."

"How long will it take?"

"I don't know."

"No," she said. "You'll just let our enemies know where we are, Ciaran."

"Dinah!" Ciaran called. "Come on, Madeline. We have to get back to the car."

"If I need to find you again, how can I do that?" Ciaran asked the man.

"No need. I will find you."

Ciaran picked Madeline up in his arms and strode away. Her mind started slipping out again, but she pulled herself back. She kept telling herself to stay focused. Think of the children. Think of their lives in Eudaiz.

Ciaran rushed back to where they had been before and found no sign of Dinah or Arik. He spun around and around. "Keep breathing, Madeline. I'm getting you back to the house." He rushed toward where they had parked the car.

As soon as they turned the corner, a group of four men appeared. She glanced at them and said, "Xiilok." He lowered her feet to the ground, leaning her against his body. He pulled out his gun with his free hand and shot. He gunned down three of them immediately. The fourth threw a knife before being shot down. Ciaran swiveled, and the knife slashed at his right shoulder.

"Must be the poor rebels. They don't even have guns," he muttered. He picked up Madeline again and rushed away. They turned another corner and were about fifty feet away from the car. Three men and a woman were walking toward them. Ciaran pulled his gun again.

"No, they're not Xiilok," she said.

He lowered the gun instantly. The people turned around, ran, and called for help. Ciaran placed her in the car. He touched her face. "Can you hang on for me, please?"

She nodded.

He ran for the driver's seat and jumped in. The next thing she knew, the car felt as if it were flying.

16

*D*inah pushed at the gate on the fence in front of Arik's house. It was a small, charming cottage tucked away in a quiet corner a few blocks away from the bridge. He towered over her and almost fell over as he handed her his keyring. "Which one..." She trailed off when he slid down to the floor and leaned against the door frame. "If you haven't touched a drop of alcohol in five years, you can just tell Ciaran. How does that bruise your ego?" she muttered as she tried the keys one by one. The ninth one was the right one.

She helped him inside the house, where he dragged himself to a couch and flopped onto it. She searched around for a light switch and couldn't find one. Then the light went on. They were standing in a small, cozy, and extremely neat kitchen. She felt like a pig when she thought about how unkempt her apartment was.

"I have tea and coffee. Please make yourself at home."

He staggered into a small hallway. She followed him.

"The reason I came here is because I need your help, Arik."

"Sure, tell me what I can do for you," he muttered with a voice still slurred with the effects of the alcohol.

"I..."

He took his shirt off in one swift move. Before she could object, his pants followed. She understood she had vomited all over him and he wanted to clean up, but he didn't have to do it right in front of her. Wait. She was the one who had followed him, and this was his house. She turned to go back to the living room.

She heard the shower start. The bathroom door wasn't closed. "I'll wait for you in the living room," she called. When she didn't hear an answer, she peeked in. He was already in the shower, so he hadn't heard her. She saw no steam in the bathroom and was surprised to think he'd be taking a cold shower in the middle of the England winter.

She turned and walked to the living room. He had identified an aperture. *Is he a jumper himself?* She absently touched the nape of her neck where the round mark was located.

A short time later, the shower water stopped running. It seemed the cold water had sobered Arik up. He walked toward the living room, wrapping a towel around his hips.

He was a beautiful creature, magnificent as he walked down the hallway toward her. She shook her head. He was human. They'd have no future together. Plus, he had a fiancée.

The closer he came, the more she could feel waves of heat coming from his body. Seeing her reaction, he approached her slowly, step by step. When he got within arm's reach, he said, "Go on...you want to do it."

She lifted her hand and placed her palm about two inches from his chest. The heat coming out of him was incredible, and his skin glowed when her palm came too close. "Wow."

He smiled. "You see, I'm literally a hot man!" He walked past her toward the couch. She looked at the nape of his neck. He had no mark. He wasn't a jumper. She let out a sigh of relief and went around to sit down on the sofa with him.

"It's not always like this. Sometimes my body just heats up. I don't know the trigger. But I guess tonight it was alcohol-related."

He waited for her questions.

"Are you human?" she asked.

"My mother would like to think so." He grinned.

"Is this some kind of special talent?"

"I wouldn't call it a talent. My body has just had an unusually high temperature since an accident. People here refer to it as being struck by lightning." He smiled.

"But it wasn't lightning, right? You just let them be comfortable with an explanation they understand."

He leaned back in the chair and looked at her. "Are you human?"

"I asked the question first."

"All right, an answer for an answer. No, it wasn't lightning. But it was something related to light."

"You found the aperture."

He gazed at her for a moment. Then he nodded. "Are you human?" he repeated.

"No. My makeup might be very close to human. But I live in Iilos, another universe, a dimension, if that makes any sense."

He smiled. "It does."

"I guess Ciaran's told you that someone is killing aperture jumpers. My friend was among those killed. I would have died, too, if I had been there." She pulled the neck of her shirt down so that he could see her mark. "Jumpers have the mark. That's the only way to identify us. I'm not here because I want to know when it's my turn to get killed. I promised my friend's mother an answer. How did you find that aperture? I need to know."

"I can't help you. I don't know. I stumbled upon it."

She buried her head in her hands. "I knew it. It had to be by chance."

They saw the beam of a flashlight shining into the house, and then there was an urgent banging on the door. Arik opened the door to see serious-looking men in uniforms surrounding his yard. "Is Dinah here?"

She approached the door. "Yes, I'm here."

The man spoke into his communication device. "Yes, sir, we found her at Arik's house." He looked at Dinah and gave her his communication divide. She picked up. It was Ciaran's voice. "Dinah, Madeline was infected by the robot bomb as well. She's dying. Do you have more antidote?"

"No. I used the strongest dose I had on you. But I can make more antidote if I have the right equipment."

"What do you need?"

"A lab."

"You've got it. Please go with my men."

"Right away."

"Can I come, too?" Arik asked.

"Yes," Ciaran answered.

Arik stormed back into the house to put some clothes on while Dinah rushed toward the car with the men.

17

The helicopter was loaded up with all of what Ciaran had asked for, and the lab was fully set up in fifteen minutes. Men in private security uniforms stormed in and out of the mansion as if they were at war. They had moved Madeline to a large room where there was medical equipment set up. She was breathing, but only with the help of a machine, and she was turning bluer by the minute. The lab was located in the adjacent room, but Ciaran wouldn't leave Madeline's side.

He rushed over to Dinah when she came in. "The lab has been set up," he said. "Can you please check to see if you need anything else?"

"Can I take a look at her?"

Ciaran nodded and stepped aside. He looked as if he was going to explode at any second.

"The machine won't help for long. I'd like you to give her this first. It will help." She gave him a needle.

"Thank you." He took the needle without hesitation and instantly injected it into a vein on Madeline's neck. It was either a sign of desperation or a complete trust in her. Dinah wasn't sure. But she didn't like having this responsibility on her shoulders. She had never made this compound in a rush with equipment she wasn't familiar with.

The door burst open and a kind old man in his late sixties entered.

"Doctor Thomas," Ciaran said and rushed toward the man, guiding him inside. "Thank you for coming on such short notice. I need you to monitor Madeline's vitals while I help Dinah with the antidote.

"For poison?" Doctor Thomas asked and took Madeline's pulse.

Ciaran nodded.

"All right, do what you have to, Ciaran. Yell out if you need a hand."

Ciaran said nothing further and took Dinah out of the room into the lab. She thought he would have flown if he could.

In the lab, he said nothing. Every movement Ciaran made was with perfect precision. As soon as she had made a batch, he tested it and ran simulations and anything else needed.

He was a thousand times better and more experienced than her in a lab. He just didn't know this compound. It made her feel a lot better to know he wouldn't just rely on her and take whatever she gave him. He understood what was going on in a lab.

She made the last batch. He tested it, and the machine gave a green signal. No matter what universe she was in, she figured green was a positive sign. She drew the compound into a needle then looked at Ciaran.

"I understand. You don't have to say it. This is the first time you made it this way, so the risk is considerable. And yes, I accept it."

What a man! she thought.

They went to the room where Madeline was. Ciaran let her handle the compound. She checked the needle carefully and then injected the antidote. She watched for Madeline's reaction and took her vitals. Then she turned around and looked at Ciaran.

She nodded.

It was as if the air in the room had been infused with lead, and now it had suddenly been lifted. It had become air again, and everyone could now breathe.

"Thank you," Ciaran said. He approached the bed, held Madeline's hand, and squeezed it slightly.

Dinah withdrew toward the door.

Doctor Thomas sat down on a chair and looked at Ciaran. Ciaran left Madeline's side and approached the doctor. He sat down on a chair opposite him. Dinah couldn't see Ciaran's face because she stood behind him. But by the expression on Doctor's Thomas's face, she knew Ciaran's held raw emotion.

"It's good to see you, son. It's been a long time," Doctor Thomas said.

Ciaran's held Doctor Thomas's hands and said nothing. Then he let go, bent down, and put his face in his hands. Dinah saw his shoulders shaking with emotion. Doctor Thomas placed his hand on Ciaran's head as if he had done it before. Like a father.

What a scene. She understood what Ciaran had been through—and that Madeline had been so close to death. But she would have never imagined the situation could shake a man like Ciaran so much.

If Madeline knew this, she wouldn't have eaten all that ice cream. Dinah rubbed her tummy.

After a while, Ciaran looked up. When he turned around and saw her, he had completely composed himself—sinfully handsome with striking gray eyes that were as cold and still as the lake in the winter castle in the highlands she had previously visited.

He approached her. "Thank you for all you've done," he said to her.

"You already thanked me."

He smiled. "I can never say it enough." He gestured toward Doctor Thomas. "This is Doctor Thomas, our family doctor."

The doctor smiled gently. "It's very impressive what a young woman like you can do these days. It makes me feel so old."

Ciaran smiled and said nothing. He gestured for them to follow him to the hall. A man in his thirties came to the door. As soon as he saw Ciaran, he rushed over.

"Jesus Christ, it seems like a decade since I last saw you." They shook each other's hands.

"Likewise. This is Dinah Greenwood. Dinah, this is Lindsay Freeman, CEO of LeBlanc Pharmaceuticals."

"It's good to see you in person." Lindsay shook her hand.

Dinah frowned.

Ciaran saw the question in her eyes and said, "I ordered a search for you."

She nodded. "It was quite a search, wasn't it? You had a whole army out looking for me."

Lindsay laughed. "We're used to this scale of operations. It's been quiet for a year. We miss it, don't we, Doctor Thomas?"

"Oh no, please leave this old man alone."

"I agree. Don't you bother Doctor Thomas unless absolutely necessary," Ciaran said, wrapping his arm around the doctor's shoulders.

"What's the damage?" Ciaran asked Lindsay.

"We have to ditch this place."

"What? Why? What about all the equipment?" Dinah asked.

Lindsay looked at Ciaran. Ciaran nodded. Lindsay explained, "Ciaran triggered quite an extensive search for you using our satellite system because we don't have any connection with you or information about you here. So that search triggered the system he uses in... other places. We have to assume his adversaries now know about this place and his whereabouts. So we're getting out now. Your credentials were also revealed during the search, Dinah."

"I'm sorry, Dinah. I wasn't thinking straight," Ciaran said.

"I don't blame you, Ciaran. Given your position, I understand the precaution is necessary. But as for me, I'm just another private investigator. It shouldn't be a problem that my identity was revealed."

Ciaran shook his head. "You're now associated with me. You're not just another investigator. Trust me, regardless of whether you want to be or not, you're now considered my people, and that puts you in danger if you're out there by yourself."

"You can't guarantee the safety of everyone you consider to be under your wings, Ciaran," Arik said, walking out from a corner.

Dinah could hear Lindsay hiss audibly. Doctor Thomas's eyes hardened as he saw Arik.

"I should have anticipated this before deciding to let him come here. I'm sorry, Lindsay," Ciaran said. He approached Arik. "You should leave now, Arik," he said.

"I won't leave without her." Arik pointed at Dinah.

"Didn't you hear what Ciaran said. It's dangerous for her to be out there by herself," Lindsay growled.

"He's not that important. I have information to help with your investigation, Dinah. Are you going with me or not?"

She nodded. "All right, I'm going with you." By all means, that was the reason she was on Earth in the first place.

"Take this." Ciaran held her hand and placed a wrist unit in her palm.

"So you can track her? Track our whereabouts?" Arik asked.

"She goes with you, she takes my unit. That's a fair deal, Arik."

"Ciaran!" Lindsay glared.

"It's okay," Ciaran said and took her to the door. At the door, he held her hand and put the wrist unit on and said, "If you need anything, my contact is coded in here. You only need to call. You are the only one who has access and can control it. If someone else takes possession of the unit, it will self-destruct. It's just a standard issue. Don't worry if you lose it."

"I'll try not to." She smiled at him then followed Arik out.

18

*T*he sun was finally shining on the charming historic city of Oxford. People began to fill the street. Shops opened and welcomed customers. Dinah checked the wrist unit Ciaran gave her and smiled. It greeted her with a smiley and asked for the passcode. She entered her secret passcode. As the screen made a ping sound of approval, she shook her head. Ciaran was a hell of a hacker. He had coded her own passcode into this machine.

She was then connected to her travel account, had her basic log, and a credit account for discrepancies. She smiled. She understood now why Ciaran had so many people working for him. He knew how to treat people. She opened her credit account and her jaw just dropped—fifty thousand credits were staring back at her. That was what he called discrepancy money? With this kind of money, she could take the first class inter-universe means of travel every day just to go grocery shopping.

"What's so funny?"

"Huh?" She looked up and saw that Arik had come back to her with two cups of coffee in his hands.

"Oh, nothing. It's just that the amount of information this little unit has is a lot more advanced than my mainframe computer in Iilos."

Arik shrugged and made no comment. "Have you had one of these before?" He handed her the coffee. "Try a sip. See if you like it."

She laughed. "We have coffee in Iilos."

"All right then."

They walked along a charming cobblestone street, heading toward his house. "Are there any of the LeBlancs that you haven't made your enemy?"

He shook his head.

"All right, so you don't want to talk about the past. It must be painful for you. So let's talk about what you promised me. What information do you have that will help my investigation?"

"I have nothing."

She choked on her coffee. "You tricked me?"

"No, I didn't trick you. I lied to you. Otherwise, you would have stayed with Ciaran."

"So because you were afraid I might become one of Ciaran's girls, you had to take me away?"

"It's for your best interest!"

"Really? I think I would be better off with Ciaran."

"They have money. That's about it. But you came all the way to Earth for your friend. I don't think you're the gold-digger kind, so being with the LeBlancs can't be beneficial for you in the long run."

"Like what happened to Juliette?"

"Don't bring her into this. You know nothing about her."

"Believe me, I know more than I need to. She used Ciaran then betrayed him."

"Of course he had to say that—"

"It wasn't him who said it. It was his current wife who said so. And she said although Ciaran never forgave anyone who betrayed him, he forgave Juliette. When they were together, there was love. And did you see what happened at the mansion with Madeline and Ciaran?"

"No."

"That was unconditional love I saw. I don't know Ciaran and Madeline at all. But I know love when I see it."

He snorted.

She jabbed her finger into his chest. "Whatever happened between you and Ciaran might run deep in the past. But from what I've seen in the last day, you're no more than a selfish, jealous prick. If you were a halfway decent man, you'd yank the stick out of your ass and help me with the investigation."

"That foreign object feels just fine where it is, so I'm going to leave it there," he snarled.

"Fine. I thought there was more to you than this. I was mistaken. It wasn't just my friend who was killed. There were many people. And there will be more if we don't stop the asshole who's doing this. I have no time to waste on you." She turned around and walked away.

"Hey!"

She kept stomping away. He pulled at her elbow. She shrugged her arm out of his grip.

"I'm sorry. I have something at the house I want to show you. It might help."

"Is this another trick?"

"No."

She gave him a warning look then walked. He followed. When they arrived at his house, Grace was waiting just outside the fence.

"What's she doing here?" Grace asked.

"I have something to show her."

"In the house?"

"Yes. of course."

"Arik, it took me two years to get inside your house. I still don't have a key. How long have you known her?"

"It's not that, Grace…"

"Then what is it?"

The wrist unit Ciaran had given Dinah buzzed. She engaged. Ciaran said, "Dinah, someone has been trying to connect to your old unit. We don't know where that unit is, but the signal bounced back from Xiilok. Someone is going to deliver a package to The Manicotti on Main Street. We think we've got our guy. It might be just the messenger. But if we can get him, dead or alive, I can trace the source to the contractor."

"Are you sure?"

"If not, I wouldn't call you. I just want you to stay clear. I've got it under control. We'll take the messenger down before he explodes the package in whatever form. No civilians will get hurt. If the signal gets to your new unit, take the call, but do *not* go to meet the messenger."

"Got it."

"All right, take care, Dinah,"

"You too." She switched off the communicator and found Arik waiting for the information while Grace paced back and forth in agitation.

"We've got to go to the market on Main Street."

She turned on the map function of her wrist unit.

"You don't need that gadget. I'll take you," Arik said.

"I'll go with you," Grace said.

Dinah shook her head.

"Okay. Grace, if you stay here, I'll come back soon, and we'll have lunch."

"Promise?"

"Yes." He kissed her forehead and charged ahead. Dinah followed. She could feel Grace glaring at her. It wasn't just a girl's jealousy in that look. It was a flash of hatred and evil—a nasty combination that she couldn't imagine coming from such a beautiful face. Had Arik ever seen this side of Grace, she wondered. Then she shook the thought away and scurried ahead.

19

*T*he market was crowded, and a sea of people walked up and down Main Street. This was the only time Dinah missed her high heels. Everyone at the market except for the children was taller than she was. Up ahead in the distance, she could see Ciaran walking toward her. He was exceptionally tall, so he stuck out like a sore thumb. She was glad he wasn't the target. Then she looked over at Arik by her side. He was tall, too. Maybe it had been a bad idea to let him come with her.

Ciaran couldn't see her, but he could see Arik. The men locked eyes with each other but said nothing. They were walking toward each other from opposite directions and were about fifty feet apart.

Suddenly she saw Ciaran's eyes darken and grow intense.

He had seen his target. He walked a little faster. He looked down, and Dinah knew he was confirming the signal on his wrist unit.

A tall man walked toward Ciaran. Although she was seeing him from behind, the tall man looked awfully familiar to her.

After confirming the signal, Ciaran looked up and straight at the man. As fast as lightning, he pulled his gun. His laser gun made no sound. But bystanders standing close by must have seen it.

Before the panic spread, Ciaran's men closed in and drove the traffic away. Because they wore uniforms, the crowd followed their instructions without question.

The tall man was hit from the front. He staggered back, his head slightly turned, before falling to the ground.

She gasped, "Cooper!"

She rushed over, but Arik grabbed her from behind.

"That's my friend. Let go of me!" She slid out of his grip and charged through the line of men in uniforms. She could see Cooper on the ground. A package was next to him.

"Cooper!"

Ciaran grabbed her. "What are you doing?"

"He's my friend!"

"He's the messenger."

"No, he's not. Let go of me." She couldn't get out of Ciaran's grip, so she started to cry.

"Let her go. Let her talk to him," Arik said.

Ciaran reluctantly let Dinah down. "Don't touch the package," he said.

She scrambled toward Cooper. "Cooper!" She brushed a stray hair from his forehead. "What are you doing here?"

He opened his eyes, groggily. "Dinah...are you okay?"

"Yes. Why are you here?"

"Just...wanted to check on you. You didn't answer your calls..." He closed his eyes.

"Please don't die, Cooper. Please look at me. I'll get you to the doctor. You'll be all right."

"So why are you crying?"

"Why are you carrying a package, Cooper?"

"What?"

"The package?"

"That's for the twenty thousand credit client. I know you didn't want me to do it, but I brought it with me in case you changed your mind..."

"Do you know these packages from Xiilok have killed people?"

"I know about it. But this one isn't a package. It a spec. I told you. I put it together as per instructions so you can see it's an easy job."

"You put this together?"

"Yes..."

"What's in it?"

"I don't know. Some fancy name."

"So you have nothing to do with the Xiiloks who are killing jumpers?"

"No...is that why you asked? You think I'm... You don't believe me? It cost five thousand credits to buy the ticket to come here...and you don't believe me."

His eyes almost rolled back.

"Please don't die. I believe you. Open your eyes for me. I'll give you back twenty thousand credits. Please don't die, Cooper."

"You don't believe me..."

"I do. Okay, watch me."

She pulled out a knife from her boot.

"No, Dinah," Ciaran shouted. Everyone jumped away. She stabbed at the package. From inside, a mound of white grains like sand poured out. She looked at the substance. "It's salt. You didn't know you packed salt?"

Cooper's voice was slurred. "I don't know jack about chemicals. It has a fancy name. Not salt."

Then she looked at Cooper's chest. "Cooper, you're not dying."

"Huh?"

She pressed her palm on his chest.

"Ouch," he moaned.

The liquid seeping out from his shirt wasn't blood. It was the substance that comprised his fake muscles, and it had neutralized the impact of the laser beam Ciaran had shot at him.

She laughed through tears. "You have a concussion, you idiot."

"Wha-a-a-t?" His voice slurred even more.

"The substance I made for your fake muscles leaked out and neutralized the effect of the beams that hit you."

"You neutralized my laser weapon with fake muscles? I am

offended. I might take back the offer I made to you," Ciaran said, looking at his gun incredulously.

She touched Cooper's face. "You know what, Cooper? I think your vanity may have just saved your life. I'll make you more fake abs. As many as you like. But please don't carry packages like this across the universes, okay?"

"Everyone sends packages everywhere. I carried it myself to save some money," Cooper muttered.

Behind her, Arik mumbled, "Courier packages. Hell..." He looked at her then Ciaran and then pulled out his cell phone.

"Jenny, where's Mother? ... She said there was a package sent to me, and I asked her to keep it for me. Where is it? ... Then go look for it ... No, no, wait ..."

She couldn't hear what the person at the other end of the line was saying. But Arik turned and looked at her, his eyes filled with fear. He rushed toward Ciaran. "Do you know how to neutralize the package if we find it? Like the one right here—if this was a real one, could you handle it?"

Ciaran stared into Arik's eyes. "No."

Arik waved his arms in the air. "So what's the point of all this?" he gestured wildly.

"It's easier if it's a bomb. I can't neutralize what I don't know. The packages might be only one form of destruction. I don't know the maker. I don't know why he did this or when he will strike again. And you could have helped if you weren't being a selfish prick. It's hit home now, and it's quite painful, isn't it? Why don't you call the US bomb squad?"

Ciaran turned and walked away.

PART II

oissy—Charles de Gaulle airport, France, 2003

ARIK GRABBED the handle on the case of his precious guitar. "No!" he said, looking at the security officer at the Roissy Charles de Gaulle airport. He'd had that guitar since he was fifteen. It had been with him for ten years—that was a lifetime relationship! There was no way he was going to let that stupid dog sniff it, lick it, or worse, scratch it.

"Non," he repeated using one of few words in his French vocabulary inventory.

The officer responded with a stream of French and pointed at the drug-detecting dog, who sat down and poked a pink tongue out from between its teeth. Arik had no problem with dogs. He might even like them. But he certainly did not like this one accusing him of carrying drugs through the airport. He didn't need this right now.

"Parlez-vous anglais?" Arik said.

"Non."

Damn it, he thought. He wished he had taken some French

lessons before traveling. The dog stood, straining at its leash to approach the case.

"Non. Non," Arik growled and pointed at the dog. And then, as the dog sat down and started thumping its tail, he said in English. "Aren't you supposed to be a passive dog? You know, the friendly kind?"

The officer didn't understand what Arik was saying. Either that or he chose to ignore what he was saying. He mangled a couple more sentences, trying to explain he didn't have a problem with his luggage being checked, but he didn't want his guitar damaged.

From the corner of his eye, he saw a young man his age step out from an area reserved for private jets and VIPs. He wore his dark hair long, tied in a ponytail at the back. He was as polished as a model straight out of a fashion magazine. But there was something about him that was incongruent with his polished model looks. Something dark, rebellious, and authoritative.

Arik's stare was long and engaging enough that the man caught his eyes. The man glanced behind him as if to see whether someone was following him.

Then the dog let out a low growl, pulling Arik's attention back to the matter at hand. He started to say, "You're not going to bark," but before he could finish, the dog barked at him.

The officer kept repeating something Arik didn't understand. But the more Arik refused, the more formal and serious the officer's tone became. The dog barked in harmony with the argument just to add to the drama.

Arik tried for the last time to communicate with the officer, but all the French words came out wrong with his thick New York accent. And with his limited knowledge of the French language, his sentences were grammatically incoherent.

Then the officer quieted down, and the dog reverted to a throaty growling. As the young man approached, he captured the officer's attention instantly. The officer shook hands with him, and Arik noticed he was a bit shaky. This young man must be someone important.

The man said something then grinned and patted Arik's shoulder as if they had been best friends in high school. The officer nodded and laughed. Arik let out as natural a laugh as possible and shoved his hands into his pockets.

The young man gestured toward the guitar case and said something. The dog let out a low bark. Arik turned toward the man and, through clenched teeth, said in English, "It's Stevie Ray Vaughan's legendary 1963 Number One Strat. It's worth $2 million. I'll burn this airport down if they put a scratch on it."

The man frowned for a brief second, glancing to a far corner. Then he looked in another direction and turned his shoulders slightly. Arik could tell he didn't want the approaching group of men in formal business suits to see him.

Arik stepped sideways to block him from their view.

The young man nodded slightly and said something else to the officer. He pointed at the dog, which stood and tried again to approach. The officer tugged on the dog's leash to make it sit down again. The dog moaned in protest. Then the officer nodded his goodbye and dragged the grumpy dog away.

Arik exhaled in relief and turned toward the young man, whose face had just turned from sunshiny summer to an icy cold winter day in a second.

"Thank you for helping out. Arik Bonneville." Arik reached his hand out for a handshake.

The man looked Arik up and down. Arik was dressed for backpacking across Europe, finally on his way to execute his turning-twenty-one dream. It was true that the twenty-one was long gone, but it was better he tried it now than never.

When he received no response from the man, Arik withdrew his hand and said, "Hey, I know you didn't really want to help me. You just wanted to avoid those jackasses in business suits. But just so you know, I don't do drugs, and I'm not carrying."

"They're not jackasses. They're my men."

There wasn't a French accent in this man's English. He had no foreign accent at all. He didn't sound British, nor did he sound American or South African or even Australian. Arik frowned. He didn't like it. He was good with accents. If someone uttered a single word, he could always tell where they came from.

"Got a name?"

The man hesitated, then said, "Ciaran."

Arik grinned. "That's a good start." He picked up his guitar. "Also, just so you know, this isn't Vaughan's guitar."

"What?"

"It's not the signature guitar worth $2 million. So don't think about robbing me!"

"Oh." Ciaran shook his head and shrugged.

"Look, I'm heading to Beynac et Cazenac." Arik pointed toward the exit.

"Have a good trip," Ciaran said quickly and turned around as if leaving. Then he saw his men coming back from that same corridor. He turned back toward Arik.

Arik chuckled. "Your stupid clothes make you stick out like a sore thumb." He tossed his hoodie at Ciaran. Ciaran grabbed it and immediately slid it on.

"Where did you say you're going?" Ciaran asked.

"Beynac et Cazenac."

"I'll take you," Ciaran said and strode quickly away.

"Ciaran!" his men called from the far end.

Ciaran darted toward the parking garage exit. Arik had only enough time to toss his bag over his shoulders, grab his guitar case, and follow Ciaran.

In the garage, Ciaran pointed the remote and pressed. A car's lights flashed.

"Well, that's beyond the caliber of an ordinary car!" Arik muttered when he saw the expensive-looking vehicle. Ciaran took Arik's hoodie off, gave it back to him, and walked over to the driver's seat. Before the car exited the garage, Ciaran's men entered. Ciaran drove straight through the gate, breaking the bar and setting off the alarm.

"Was that necessary?" Arik asked.

"No," Ciaran said, his eyes as cold as steel. "But you don't want to get caught, do you?"

"Dude, I told you, I'm not carrying anything I need to worry about. I traveled to Asia before coming here. My luggage must have traces of a drug of some sort. I just didn't want the dog to scratch my guitar..." He trailed off as the hand he had underneath the hoodie Ciaran had just given back to him hit a plastic bag. He pulled it out. Inside the bag was a capped syringe containing blue liquid.

"Jesus Christ, *you* were carrying. The dog was barking at you! You used me, dickhead."

The car had entered the highway. Ciaran veered off onto a smaller road.

"It's not a drug. It's a rare medicine," Ciaran said.

"So why did you run?"

"I didn't say it was legal!"

"Those jackasses are your own people. Why are you running from them?"

A storm was coming. Lightning streaked across the darkening sky. Ciaran looked up at the clouds and then accelerated along the country road which had started to muddy due to the rain and poor drainage.

"Slow down, will you?"

Ciaran ignored him. He glanced at the rearview mirror and saw the silhouette of a car chasing them. His eyes darkened, and he accelerated even more.

"Did you steal the meds from those guys?"

Ciaran shook his head. "No one wants to be in possession of this, trust me. It's extremely poisonous."

Arik dropped the bag.

Ciaran glanced at him. "If compounded correctly, it can heal rare diseases. What you are holding is a healing compound."

"Right. Then why are you running? And please slow down!"

"It's my family's formula. Our French business counterparts didn't like the healing compound. They wanted the narcotic formula."

"Why can't they have theirs and you have yours?"

"They want mine because I destroyed the last narcotic sample they got before I left."

Arik laughed. Ciaran smiled, but the smile faded quickly from his face when they saw a whirl of light ahead. Ciaran hit the brakes, but the momentum of the car still sent them straight into the light.

Then everything turned white.

21

*A*rik opened his eyes groggily. Eric Clapton's voice singing "Crossroads" echoed in his head. The voice kept repeating the desperate verse, "*I went down to the crossroads...fell down on my knees.*" He closed his eyes, trying to shake the song off. It did go silent for a second. Then Queen's "Bohemian Rhapsody" blasted out without warning. He closed his eyes again, and the music went off.

"He's back!" He heard Dinah's voice, and the music stopped completely. He would never have thought she'd be his anchor to reality. The memories came rushing back. He was at the market, trying to get his sister to look for his mother. Then the phone went dead. He'd had no choice but to go back to New York. Since Ciaran had refused to help, he'd hoped to get a standby ticket at the airport. He took shortcuts down a few small roads, hoping to get to the M40 motorway quickly so that he could get to the airport in under forty minutes. While driving, he dialed his sister's number several times without success.

Bam! He hit something. Or something hit him. Then his world went completely blank.

He opened his eyes to find Dinah's witty face hovering over his.

"How are you feeling?" she asked.

He loved her eyes. Large, dark, focused, and full of secrets. Her pouting lips always made him want a taste. And for some unexplainable reason, he knew he would love to hear that Irish accent of hers for the rest of his life.

"What happened?" Arik asked.

"It looks like you had a car accident."

He blinked. He wasn't lying in his car, but on a stretcher. He guessed he was in an ambulance. He had been trying to go to the airport. *Mother!* He sat right up.

"Hey, that's okay. Ciaran has it under control," Dinah said.

"What?"

"He's got someone locating your family in the US."

Arik nodded. Having money came in handy sometimes. Ciaran could afford to have the entire universe working for him, Arik thought. "How did you find me?"

"I didn't. Ciaran did."

Arik buried his head in his hands. *How many more times would he have to hear Ciaran's name?*

The man himself approached. "Tell me you're okay, and I'll ask the paramedics to let you leave without going to the hospital," Ciaran said.

Arik looked up from his hands. "I'm fine. If I have to go back to the hospital again, I'll have to make it my permanent address."

Ciaran nodded and turned away to talk to the paramedics.

Arik asked Dinah, "How did he find me?"

Dinah shrugged and shoved her hand into his jacket pocket. She pulled out a small round black chip the size of a lemon seed.

"You bugged me?"

"It's Ciaran's device, part of the wrist unit he gave me. So in principle, he found you."

Arik hopped off the stretcher and exited the ambulance. "Normally I'd say I don't like having my privacy invaded, and I make that known. But I need to go now, and that bug may actually have saved me. So let's consider things even."

She raised an eyebrow. "Even? Between you and me, or between you and Ciaran?"

Arik shook his head and muttered, "He and I will never be even."

"What?"

"Never mind." He walked away from the ambulance and looked at what was left of the car. He wondered how he had survived a crash like that. He looked down at his hands and then his body. He barely had a scratch on him.

He turned and was about to ask Dinah more questions when he saw the shadow of the yellow-eyed man among the trees in the distance. He swallowed a curse and looked away. The man must have yanked him out of the car before the impact. He had to protect his gift in Arik.

Ciaran approached after sending the paramedics away. Arik raised an eyebrow, gesturing toward the ruin of his car. "So people just go away without question just because you tell them to?"

Ciaran cast a glance at him. "Pretty much."

Arik waved his arms in the air, about to let out the nastiest remark he could think of, but he decided against it. "Thanks for your help. Dinah said you're looking for my family?"

"You're welcome. But you sound a little like you're pulling your teeth out right now." Ciaran glanced at his wrist unit. "We found Jenny, and my men are bringing her here. She's on our private jet, so she's safe."

Arik shoved his hands in his pants pockets. "Thank you."

Ciaran nodded. "We searched, but we couldn't locate the package in the house. And we still can't find Diana."

Arik shook his head. "They've got Mother and the package. Why her? She has nothing to do with this."

"They want you. So they'll use Diana to lure you out. Any idea what they want from you apart from the illusion that you've identified the pattern of the aperture occurrences?"

"No, I didn't identify it. I bumped into it accidentally."

"And he's not a jumper," Dinah added.

"He told you that?"

"He doesn't have the mark of a jumper."

Ciaran said nothing.

"So we're waiting for them to contact me to say exactly what they want?" Arik asked.

Ciaran nodded. "I've got to get back to our place."

"How's Madeline?" Arik asked.

"Thanks for asking. She's recuperating." Ciaran turned to walk away.

"I'm sorry," Arik said.

Ciaran turned back. "Me too."

Dinah frowned but said nothing.

esches, France, 2003

ARIK GRABBED the car seat as it spun into the dome of light. He looked over at Ciaran. The man didn't even blink as he did his best to control the car. This guy's nerves must be made of steel, Arik thought. As they spun, Arik realized they weren't headed into a dome of alien light but rather into a row of trucks shining headlights at them from across the field just off the D45A.

"Cover your head," Ciaran said.

Arik did so instantly, just before the car hit something and came to an abrupt stop. The airbag inflated into his face, making him see thousands of stars.

"Get out of the car," Ciaran said.

Arik unbuckled the seatbelt and dove outside. As soon as they had rolled clear and scrambled to their feet, the car exploded. "There goes my guitar!" Arik muttered in disbelief.

There was some movement to their left. Before Arik had a chance to turn to see what it was, he heard Ciaran yell, "Get down!" Arik dropped himself down to the ground, lying flat on the mud.

Ciaran darted toward a tree trunk to take cover and pulled out two handguns. Arik could see a group of men, all of them brandishing guns, walking toward them from the trucks in the distance. There were too many. He wasn't sure Ciaran could handle this.

Before the group of men moved any closer, shots were fired from behind the group of men. They turned and began exchanging fire with their attackers.

Ciaran said, "We'll have to run into the bush. Let them cancel each other out. How fast can you run?"

"For my life? I could win an Olympic medal!"

"Okay, run to the right. On three."

Arik nodded. Ciaran looked back at the fighting men, braced against the tree to prepare, then signaled the count to three. Arik hopped up from the ground, and they both ran into the woods.

There was shouting. Some of the men had seen them running away, but they continued to fire at one another.

Ciaran and Arik had run for a while. It seemed they had escaped the situation. Ciaran pulled out his cell phone and called someone. He spoke in English, so Arik figured he was speaking to one of his men, not the French business counterparts who were chasing them. He finished the conversation quickly, then said to Arik, "We have to get out of the bush. There's no way my men can navigate in here."

Ciaran pulled out the plastic bag with the blue syringe and checked for damage.

"Bloody hell. Guns. Goons. And drugs. Give me one reason *not* to think you're a drug dealer."

Ciaran shrugged. "I told you. This isn't a drug. It's a healing compound. It's true we're in the pharmaceutical business, but I wouldn't say drug dealing is the correct business description."

"That drug will get us killed. So you'd better make sure it can save lives or cure cancer or something like that."

"It can do more than that."

"Yeah, right."

Suddenly two men charged at them from the bush. Ciaran gave Arik a hard kick to his abdomen, sending him to the ground. He pulled his guns out and fired at the attacking men. The exchange was fast, and the two men went down like tree trunks.

As Arik lay on the muddy ground, he felt a puncture on his neck, and then his world started to fade.

Ciaran crouched down and reached out his hand. "Come on up. I didn't kick you that hard."

Ciaran was moving so slowly—or maybe it was because Arik's world was starting to blur, and things seemed to be moving in slow motion. He tried to say something about the pain in his neck, but no words came out.

Ciaran muttered some profanity and took a closer look at him. He turned Arik's head, swore, and pulled something out of his neck. Standing, he ground whatever it was into the ground with his foot.

Arik felt tired. He thought maybe he should rest for a bit. Then he felt a slap on his face.

"Stay awake, will you?" said Ciaran.

Damn it, he just wanted to sleep for a while. As soon as he closed his eyes, Ciaran shook his shoulders violently. "Open your eyes. If you die, no drug will be able to help you."

He opened his eyes and saw Ciaran had pulled off the cap of his blue syringe. He tapped lightly at a vein on Arik's neck and injected some of the blue medicine.

Arik felt the cool liquid flow into his body and mind—a stream of life. He felt the light and spark of an inexplicable source of energy flood his body. He had never before had a clarity like this in his mind. It felt as if he was transforming into a different person.

In a short moment, he snapped back to reality and sat up. Two dead bodies lay on the ground, and Ciaran was sitting down, leaning against a tree.

"Feeling like a superman now?" Ciaran asked.

Arik touched his neck where he had felt the pain before.

Ciaran chuckled. "You were stung by a scorpion in France in the wet season. I think you should buy a lotto ticket."

"You injected me with that blue drug!"

"Consider yourself a very lucky Guinea pig. It worked. You should buy *two* lotto tickets..." His voice trailed off.

Arik rushed over to him and saw blood seeping out from between the fingers of the hand Ciaran was clutching at his side. A lot more blood had pooled up on the ground, and Ciaran was white as a sheet.

"You've been shot."

"My men are coming soon," Ciaran muttered with his eyes closed.

"Are you sure they can find us in here?"

"No. But as you can see, I can't carry you out."

"Idiot. You could have left me here."

No response from Ciaran.

Arik shook his shoulder. "Hey! Let's get out of here." He hauled Ciaran up off the ground and wrapped his arm around his shoulders. "Okay, one step at a time. You've got to help me out here," Arik said.

Ciaran slumped to the ground. Arik straightened him up and took one more step. "Come on, we have to make it out of the woods. Now that you know your drug works, you have to get it out there. Save lives, right? Cure cancer. Be God!"

"I don't want to be God. His job sucks." Ciaran's voice slurred, and he slumped down again.

He must have lost a lot of blood, Arik thought. "Whatever. Okay, you can tell me the formula. That way, if you die here, I'll tell your people, whoever they might be."

"LeBlanc Pharmaceuticals."

"Okay, good, keep walking. LeBlanc Pharmaceuticals. And what's in the drug?"

"Oleander."

"What's that?"

"It's a flower."

"A what?"

Before Ciaran could say anything more, they heard footsteps.

"Could that be your men? How can I tell?"

Ciaran pulled out a gun and gave it to Arik. "Have you ever fired a gun before?"

"In video games."

"If they're my men, they won't fire at us. But if they look like they're going to shoot, you have to do it first. Aim at the head..." He slumped down again.

Two men walked out from the woods. In the dim light of near dusk, Arik saw them pulling guns. He was outnumbered. Ciaran was totally out of it on the ground. He had to think fast. No—he didn't have time to think. He swung the gun up and fired two shots. The men fell before they knew what had hit them.

It was Arik's first kill.

hey had moved Madeline to a new location. Dinah could see it was much more secure than the previous place. She appreciated Ciaran allowing Cooper to stay inside to recover.

Arik had said nothing on the way to the location. She knew he had a lot on his mind, and she was still pondering the odd conversation he'd had with Ciaran. Whatever had happened in the past must have scarred their relationship badly, like an unhealable wound. She didn't think Madeline even knew about it.

As soon as they arrived, Ciaran had made a beeline to the bedroom. Dinah went to check on Cooper, but he was asleep. She went to her room and saw her ruined jumpsuit in a plastic bag. She took the suit out. Ciaran hadn't merely fixed it—this was a new suit that looked more like a jacket than the skintight suit she'd had before. This would be warmer, and she could tuck more weapons inside.

She put the suit back into the bag and took it to the living room, where she found Arik standing by himself and staring out the window. Approaching him, she asked, "Want to help me with this?"

He turned around and smiled, but the smile didn't reach his eyes.

She pointed at the bag. "My new weaponry suit."

Arik nodded without enthusiasm.

"Look, I know you're worried, but Ciaran is very confident they won't harm your mother until they get what they want from you."

"What if I can't give them what they want?"

"So you know what they want?"

"I should call Grace. I didn't come back to the house to have lunch with her as I'd promised. It's been a few hours. She must be worried sick."

"Arik, that was yesterday."

"What?"

"We went to the market, and Cooper was shot. Ciaran brought Cooper back here. Then we didn't hear from you. He put out a search for you, and that activated the chip I planted in your pocket. But that was yesterday."

"I had planned to get to the airport in under forty minutes. Yes, I had an accident, but that couldn't have been yesterday."

Ciaran approached them from the corridor. "What's up?" he asked.

"Arik lost a day."

"I just left the market for the airport. How is it possible that I was hanging around all night without knowing it?"

Ciaran's wrist unit beeped, and he engaged.

A voice said, "Report of a possible attack last night on the outskirts of Oxford."

"In what form?" Ciaran asked.

"Fire sparked by lightning."

"Casualties?"

"Twenty humans."

"No creatures?"

"We can't confirm, sir."

"Why are you concluding it's a supernatural incident?"

"Our device picked up traces of multiversal energy in the affected areas. Local authorities are working to identify the site. We can't get any more information until the humans are cleared from the area, sir."

"All right. Keep me informed," Ciaran said and hung up.

"Was that me? Did I do that?" Arik asked. "How could that happen? I haven't even had the second heatwave yet!"

Ciaran narrowed his eyes. "So you've had your first one? When was it?"

"After you guys got drunk and had a fistfight on the street," Dinah said. "So what happens? You have a certain number of heatwaves like that, and you turn into lightning?"

"I don't know. It can't be me!" Arik exclaimed.

"It's not you," Ciaran said. "The last thing we need now is you freaking out."

"You never knew what it was that I could do—or could have done." Arik turned and walked toward the door.

Ciaran grabbed him from behind. "If you leave, we'll never figure it out."

Arik whirled around. "Don't grab me! There's nothing you can do even if we do figure it out. And you don't have to figure out anything anyway. It wasn't your fault." He walked away once more.

Ciaran grabbed his shoulder again. Arik threw a punch, and Ciaran caught his fist. "I left you alone in the past, Arik. But that was a lifetime ago, and you still can't deal with it. So let's sort it out now."

Arik shoved Ciaran away.

Ciaran grabbed his collar and pushed him against the wall. "It *is* my fault. And I'm going to fix it whether you like it or not so that you can go on and live your selfish life however you want."

"Selfish? Are you saying I didn't try? I went through regression hypnosis. I tried every kind of psychiatric test shit available on Earth. And they had no clue what's going on."

"Can someone fill me in?" Dinah asked.

Ciaran looked at Arik, then at Dinah. "I think you might be able to help. He was stung by a rare poisonous scorpion. To save his life, I injected him with a new healing compound I developed. It was made primarily from oleander, a toxic Earth flower. He claims there's a side effect of the compound that makes him time travel whenever he experiences three heatwaves. He has no memory of the events whatsoever but says he always causes something catastrophic to happen when he travels."

"When I travel to the past, that is," Arik growled. "Ciaran's never seen any of my heatwaves. But you did, Dinah."

"It never happened when I was around. I can't babysit you," said Ciaran. "If you would have allowed my experiment, I could have triggered a heatwave and measured it. We could have had a solution a long time ago."

"I am not your lab rat. And I've had it under control. I stopped it five years ago."

"And that was about the time you stumbled upon the apertures?" Ciaran chuckled. "It seems you jumped out of the frying pan into the fire."

Arik staggered back, leaning against the wall. "Why are the heatwaves coming back? I can't afford to time travel now. They've got my mother. I have to be here. I can't control it. What if I never come back?" He was breathing heavily. "I need to be alone." He shoved Ciaran out of the way and rushed down the hallway.

Ciaran felt the shoulder where Arik had just touched him and said to Dinah, "He's heating up now. He told me the second one is worse than the first." He looked at Arik, who was at the end of the hall. "Hey, Madeline's in there!" But Arik had already slammed the door shut and locked it from the inside.

$\mathcal{M}$adeline bolted out of the bed when Arik stormed in. She had heard the commotion outside and was prepared to go out to check. She thought she was recovered, but Ciaran was overly cautious and insisted she stay for one more day.

Arik's face was as pale as a ghost, but the skin on his face was the only part of him that didn't look like it was burning. For the first time since they had met, she could read his mind. What she heard was horrifying. It didn't sound like speech. Distorted, mangled words merged together as if space creatures were holding a conversation. Some of the words seemed to be in English, and there was a kind of rhythm or beat weaving in and out of the words.

Her psychic ability wasn't useful now because she couldn't make sense of what she was hearing.

He was surprised to see her, but he was out of breath and couldn't utter a word to explain why he had stormed into her room.

Ciaran banged on the door. Madeline knew Ciaran's extreme concern regarding her security had just bitten him in the backside. For her safety, he had coded the door so that if it were locked from the inside, no one—including him—could break in from the outside.

Arik leaned against the wall then slid down to the floor.

She approached him and could feel the incredible heat coming from his body. His eyes were glassy. Ciaran could help. She darted toward the door to open it for her husband. Arik grabbed her foot as she walked past, sending her to the floor.

"Don't. He can't help," Arik said.

"I can't help either, Arik. And you look like you need some help."

"This is the second and...the third combined... It's never happened this way before..." His eyes rolled back.

"Second and third what?"

He closed his eyes.

"If I don't come back...please tell my mother...I'm sorry..."

"Hey!" Madeline grabbed him by the shoulders before he fell to the floor. As she did so, she heard Ciaran's voice coming from outside the door.

"Don't touch him, Madeline, whatever you do!"

She looked back at Arik and saw his image flicker. Her hands, which still gripped his shoulders, also flickered. Then the world went blank.

In a flash, Madeline found herself standing next to Arik in the middle of a busy coastal port. It was grim and dark as if a storm had just moved past. People rushed around, going about their business, and no one paid attention to the fact they had just appeared out of nowhere and were dressed like no one else around them.

"We're in the fourteenth century," Arik said.

"What?"

"On your right is the port of a seacoast line, a busy trading business because shipping goods by water is more affordable in the middle ages."

Madeline looked toward the port. Boats with single sails were moored to the dock, where people raced about carrying goods in containers, parcels, and cages. Hearing a quack and a high-pitched squeal next to her, Madeline jumped and moved aside as a man wearing a dirty knee-length tunic and thick shoes and pushing a cart of live animals walked past.

"Up the hill, you might be able to see some carriages," Arik continued. "People of their class dress a bit nicer. Those of prestige won't come near the dock."

Madeline looked up the hill. It was exactly as Arik had described. As she looked back at him, he shrugged and said, "I specialize in the history of the middle ages."

"Ciaran said you specialized in mythology."

He chuckled. "What can I say? I have multiple interests."

"So what's next, Arik? This isn't our time, so it's obvious we've time traveled. How do we get back? It seems like you've done this before."

He smiled. "Once or twice." His smile was so sad it worried her. Not only did she want to get back to her own time, she also wanted to get back to her universe, to Eudaiz, where her children were waiting.

"I don't know what will happen to you, Madeline. But whenever this happens to me, I can't remember a thing when I get back. I am fully aware of what I'm doing now. And I know what I did on my last trip. I know I'll feel really bad when I get back—but I never know why."

She nodded. "As long as we can get back."

"We can always go back, but the question is—in what state."

"I don't know anything about time travel, Arik, but I know one thing—we're not supposed to change the past. Things happen for a reason. The universe operates in a sequence of cause and effect. It's all a big chain reaction. If we change anything in this time, things will be changed when we get back, and it might not be a good change."

"You sound exactly like Ciaran, Madeline."

She shrugged. "We're married. You hadn't noticed?"

"This time travel happens for a reason. I know whenever I traveled in the past, something catastrophic happened. I never know why, and I can never remember if I did something to cause changes to occur."

"Where did you go in your last travel?"

"1931. The China flood. It killed millions. I saw it happen with my own eyes. I don't know if I did something to cause it. I did bring a vase back with me—a rare antique that proves I was there. But still, I can't remember what I did. I meant to show that vase to Dinah. But we didn't have time."

"Maybe we should find a discreet corner and wait there for the right time to return. You promise you won't do anything drastic?"

Arik nodded. They walked across the dirt road and stood at the corner of what looked like a small trading station. On a low bench outside the place lay a range of butcher knives and other tools of slaughter.

Madeline rolled her eyes. "How charming!" she said and tugged Arik's arm, hoping to find another place to wait. Before they had a chance to leave, a man stepped up to them from the dock. He looked Madeline up and down. She knew her face was feminine enough, but she was wearing jeans, not exactly the style of clothing women wore in that era. Arik pulled her back behind him and gave the man a stern stare.

The man grinned, showing his crooked teeth. "Flowers for the beautiful lady."

She noticed now that he was carrying a large basket full of all sorts of flowers. Most of them looked like wildflowers, pulled from a field nearby. Maybe he was taking the flowers to the market. He pulled out some purple flowers and handed them to Madeline. As she accepted them, he nodded with respect, and then walked away.

Arik grabbed the flowers and threw them to the ground.

"They're just flowers, Arik!"

"I'll buy you buckets of them when we get back."

From around the corner, they heard men's voices.

"Thank you very much for your understanding. Here is a token of my appreciation." The voice had a thick French accent. Arik peeked around the corner and saw that the French man had left.

A man in an officer's uniform stood, counting gold coins in a pouch. A younger man approached in a hurry, and the man in uniform quickly slid the coins into his pocket.

The younger man said, "We shouldn't allow those French ships to dock at Dorset port, sir. They've been to the East before coming here. They might be carrying unwanted goods, sir."

"Frenchmen? I don't think so, son. They have only silk on board."

"They've told you so, sir?"

"No, I checked myself. Now, you go and check on the ones coming from up the coast. I am worried more about them."

"Are you sure?"

"How long have you been working here?"

"Four weeks, sir."

"All right, I've been here five years. Do you understand?"

"Yes, sir."

"Get out of my sight."

The younger officer scurried away.

Arik ground his teeth and reached for a butcher knife. Madeline grabbed his hand.

"What is it, Arik? Talk to me."

"This is Dorset in 1348. For a few gold coins, that greedy bastard is going to let the French boats in. One of those boats launched the beginnings of the Black Death—the plague that wiped out more than half of England's population. If I shove this knife down his throat right now, it will save half of England."

25

*C*iaran nearly bulldozed the door. He stormed into the room, but Arik and Madeline were nowhere to be found. Dinah knew the two had time traveled. Ciaran was calm compared to the time when Madeline had almost died and he'd had no hopes of saving her. Maybe it was because she was with Arik, and Arik had apparently made it back to this modern time before without fail. Ciaran paced the room even though he knew it wouldn't help.

"One signal from her. That's all I need. I could trace that."

"Are you talking to me?" Dinah asked.

"I beg your pardon?"

"Were you talking to me?"

"I'm sorry, no. Well actually, yes. You were at Arik's place. Did you see anything I could use to trace where he might have traveled to?"

"I might—"

Ciaran's wrist unit beeped, and he engaged instantly.

"Your guest from New York has arrived, sir."

"I'll be right there." Then he looked at Dinah. "That's Jenny, Arik's sister."

"Right...sure. We can talk on the way," she said and strode out of the room. In the corridor, she slammed into Cooper.

"Ouch. Watch where you're going, lady." He grinned, and his eyes sparked recognition as he saw Ciaran.

Before Cooper could say anything, Ciaran cut in, "I didn't know you were Dinah's friend. You bounced signals from Xiilok to her device, and you carried a package. Next time, before you travel the multiverse, take care that you don't look like a multiversal terrorist. Fake muscles won't be able to save you from my advanced weapons."

Cooper's eyes widened. "Y-you're Eudaizian? You're—"

"Cooper," Dinah warned.

Ciaran shoved his hands into his pockets, raising an eyebrow in challenge.

"I know weapons," said Cooper. "You shot me with a Eudaizian gun. Without authorization, no one can operate their advanced weapons. And authorization works on individual IDs. Even spouses in Eudaiz don't share IDs." He moved closer.

"Stop it, Cooper," Dinah warned again.

"No, let him," Ciaran said. "I'd like to see how good of an investigator your partner is. You have three minutes, Cooper."

Cooper grinned. "The gun you use fires nine round beams simultaneously at a speed faster than light. You can control the damage it inflicts by deducing the density of the beam and whether you would add other damaging sources to it. What you gave me was pure laser beams, the lowest dose. If you had combined it with your natural energy, I would have been dead. Most importantly, that gun is only available to people of councillor rank in Eudaiz."

Ciaran smiled. "A level one hacker could extract that information from the multiversal database. A private investigator with a specialized license could gain access to the information at an even higher level. We're leaving, Dinah."

Cooper nodded. "Fair enough. You're a high-ranking Eudaizian councillor. Based on your shot accuracy, you must be in the combat group. But to get my bounced signals, you also have to be comfortable with intelligent technology. So you also have to be in the brainy group. You're an all-rounder, and that's what propelled you to the top of the Eudaizian council."

Ciaran shrugged, still walking away.

"The majority of the council, especially those at the Sciphil rank, have British and Irish origins," Cooper continued.

Ciaran turned around. "What does Sciphil stand for?"

"Scientist Philosopher—derived from Earth English. Obviously! Just like Iilos tries to be like Ireland, the Eudaizian council tries to put as many memories of their time on Earth in their chamber as possible."

Ciaran advanced toward Cooper. "What else do you know?"

Cooper stepped back but continued. "Native Eudaizians have light hair color. Even though they can change their profiles and appearance, your appearance isn't a profile—it's a natural look. And that makes you the one and only person I can think of—you're Ciaran LeBlanc." Cooper had backed into a wall and couldn't move back any further. "You're Ciaran LeBlanc, king of Eudaiz and one of the two Irish bloodlines running in the council."

Ciaran pulled his knife and held it to Cooper's throat. "And what's the other bloodline?"

"The Flanagans. They've finished, of course. It dated back to the 1500s, Earth time. But they were in the council."

"You're a hacker. Who do you work for?" Ciaran growled, pressing his knife harder. A drop of blood from Cooper's neck beaded at the tip of the knife.

Dinah darted in front of Cooper. "Cooper barely remembers his passcode, Ciaran. He's an excellent investigator, but he's harmless. Trust me. We're freelance. We don't work for anyone."

"Information about the Flanagans is only available in one databank. No one of any caliber could hack it."

"I didn't hack anything." Cooper's voice was a bit shaky now seeing the tenacity in Ciaran's eyes.

"Ciaran, he doesn't have that skill. Hacking is my department," Dinah said.

"You don't read minds, do you, Dinah?" Ciaran asked.

"No."

"So you don't know what he really knows."

"Trust me, technology doesn't agree with me at all, and I didn't have to hack. That's public information."

"What?" Ciaran snarled.

Cooper raised his hands. "I apologize. I'm sorry if that information is sensitive. I've always wanted to emigrate to Eudaiz, so I did my homework. The dynamics in your council and the bloodlines come from my deductions. I searched a public network for common surnames that originated from Earth and put that together with a few other bits and pieces. But all of that is free, public info from the network."

"What network?"

"Toogle."

"What?" Ciaran exclaimed.

"You *Toogled* this?" Dinah chuckled.

"Yes, you can find a lot of information there. You should try it sometime. But it takes a talented brain to make sense of the information. Otherwise, it's just an ocean of mumbo jumbo."

Ciaran withdrew his knife. "What is Toogle?"

Dinah said, "It's like the Earth system they call the Internet. But this one is multiversal. It's not a databank. It's an open-sourced information portal."

"Are there many networks like this available? Can you identify them?"

Cooper grinned. "There are a handful. I use them often. They're my bread and butter. I can't hack or use a formal databank like Dinah."

Ciaran nodded. "Good. You can come with me." He strode away.

Cooper grabbed Dinah's elbow. "Is that a job offer I just heard?"

She chuckled. "In your dreams, Cooper," she said and scurried after Ciaran.

26

*D*iana opened her eyes, feeling a bit groggy, and saw the
back of the man who was holding her captive. He was tall
and looked strong. But she was sure he had a weak spirit. No strong
man would hold an old woman like her for ransom. She knew her
son wouldn't give in to whatever this man wanted. He must have
drugged her. Coward! She felt embarrassed for his parents, whoever
they may be.

She missed her son terribly—not just the twenty-something Arik,
who was born to be free and wild, but the whole of him. He was her
son, and she accepted him no matter how he had changed or what he
had become. If only he had told her what trouble he was dealing
with.

He loved music and travel. That was his life. She would never
forget the day he'd come back after his trip to Europe. Something
terrible had happened, and it had changed him. He'd abandoned his
music and delved into serious studies of subjects she had never heard
of. Then he'd moved to England. The fact that he turned into a
serious academic didn't rob Diana of her son, but the distance he had
put between them did.

He made a new friend over there—Ciaran LeBlanc. She was glad he had someone he could confide in. Ciaran dropped in to visit her whenever he had business in New York. The strange thing was that there was a period of time when Ciaran had visited her more than her own son.

She loved Ciaran like a second son. But there was a secret corner in his mind she could never get to—one he wouldn't let anyone get to. There was something dark and broken in him. She thought one day she would like to get both Arik and Ciaran together, clear the air, and get them to behave like her good sons. But the next thing she knew, Arik and Ciaran were fighting over a girl, and that ended their friendship. She hadn't seen Ciaran since then.

The man turned around, and she instantly closed her eyes and pretended she was still unconscious. She heard him dial the phone and talk to someone in a language she didn't know. The voice of this man was the weirdest thing she had ever heard in her life. It was hollow, and it echoed as if he was making noise rather than speaking.

She had heard that noise before. Yes, it was when Jenny had had friends over for her eighteenth birthday. They had been watching the classic Arnold Schwarzenegger movie, *Predator*. The slimy green-black alien in that movie made the same sound. But that was just a movie. In front of her was reality.

She heard his footsteps outside the room. She moved her arms, which were tied loosely behind her back. The man must have thought she was a defenseless old woman and tied her up for precaution only. She easily pulled her hands out of the rope. She hadn't reached her sixtieth birthday yet, so she was effectively still a very proud fifty-something-year-old woman.

She had retired, but her years as an aikido sensei had not been wasted. She was still as fit, strong, and agile as she had been when she was younger. Arik had gotten his musical genes from his father, not from her. Now she was about to break the bones of those who were trying to hurt her son.

She lay still and waited. The kidnapper returned to the room. She opened her eyes and looked at him. She smiled. He didn't smile back. How rude! She sat up from the floor, keeping her hands behind her back so he didn't know she had broken loose from the rope.

He approached and crouched in front of her. As soon as he got within range, she swiveled her legs, stood up in a flash, and pivoted so that she stood behind him.

He jumped up to his feet and turned around. She pivoted again to position herself behind him. He was very tall and bulky around the shoulders, but that was no problem for her. The stronger he was, the heavier he was, and the harder he was going to fall if he attacked her. That was the key principle of aikido defense.

He turned around again to face her and moved his hand to his side to get his gun.

Now that was a situation she referred to as the last drop. When a coward cheated, there was nothing to redeem him in her eyes.

"Stop, I don't want to have to hurt you," Diana said.

He continued to reach for his gun. Before his hand touched the barrel, she whirled around to his side and grabbed a couple of his fingers.

She heard cracks, and he roared in pain. That was about right—the sound of broken bones in the fingers. She pulled his gun and pointed it at him as he was about to charge at her.

"This is your second warning. If you move, I'll shoot."

He ignored her warning.

She didn't shoot. She didn't like guns, and she didn't need them. She lowered her body and topped him over her shoulders. He tipped over to the back of her, head first. His body weight became the lethal weapon she used against him. She heard another crack. This time, it was from his neck.

She stood over the dead man. "I would have given you a chance to apologize for kidnapping me, but I doubt you know any etiquette." Then the dead man started to melt, and his body turned into a puddle of swimming worms right before her eyes. She yelped and jumped aside.

Soon there was nothing left but worms on the floor.

Figuring the cops wouldn't be able to identify the man—or the thing—she decided to leave the remains. She saw the package that had been sent to Arik on the table. They must have snatched it at the same time they kidnapped her.

She grabbed it and left the room.

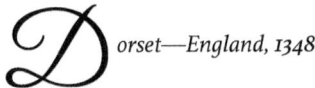 *orset—England, 1348*

MADELINE PULLED on Arik's elbow to stop him from heading around the corner to confront the officer who had just received a bribe to allow the French ships into Dorset. He was tall and strong, and he slid out of her grip twice. He was so angry she could feel the rage ebbing out from him in waves. This was so much like Ciaran's rage—primal and uncontrollable. But Ciaran had a way of redirecting the energy of his rage into his mind blades. The blades directed by his mind could dig up a hillside and kill hundreds. Arik didn't seem to be able to control his anger.

"I have to kill him. I have to stop this! I can stop the Black Death," Arik growled, pacing back and forth.

Madeline shook her head. "You're talking about two different things. Yes, you can kill this man, Arik. But that doesn't mean you'll stop the plague. The plague is—it *was*—something that happened. It's a fact we know. If you kill him, the plague will still happen, but by causes unknown to us. Or a pandemic worse than the plague might occur. Do you want to be responsible for that?"

"I time traveled for a reason. I was sent here for a reason, Madeline. Millions of people will die if I do nothing. True, something worse might happen if I stop this one. But that's just speculation, isn't it? What if whatever happens in place of the plague is a lesser threat?"

"To repeat your point, Arik, that's speculation. So we either deal with fact, or we deal with speculation. I prefer to stick with the facts. We know what happened in the past, and we'll find a solution to deal with it in the future. I don't like the idea of us taking chances shooting at moving goal posts."

"So you expect me to do nothing? I'm sure I've killed before. I'm sure that whenever I traveled to the past, I was sent to places at exactly the times when significant things were about to happen. I know I would have done something about it."

"And then what?"

"When I come back to the present, I remember nothing. I think I forget for a reason."

"Oh, so now you think you're some kind of vigilante who can take matters into his own hands and doesn't have to face the consequences of what he does?"

"For your information, I cop the consequences big time. Whenever I come back, I don't remember what I did or where I went. But I always know I have blood on my hands, regardless of whose it is. You tell me—remembering or not remembering... which one is worse?"

He slammed his palms against the wall outside the trading station.

"You were alone before. But this time, you're with me. And I can remember."

"How?"

"I'm only half human. Ciaran must have told you that."

"I know now."

"I'm a psychic, a mind reader, and a mind tracker. Now you know that, too. My mind doesn't work the same way as yours. I do remember, and I'll tell you when we get back whether you killed someone or changed the course of history. I'll tell you if you've caused something worse to happen."

"Really?"

"Yes. So do you think you can you stop yourself from killing this time?"

He nodded.

They heard a crash and then a cry from inside the station. Madeline peeked through a small gap in the wooden wall and saw the old officer grabbing a poor young female peasant's breasts. The girl cried, but her cry was quickly muffled by the man's hand.

"Easy. Don't cry. I'll pay you. You don't have to go to the market with this stale bread today."

"Please, sir...please let me go. The bread is freshly baked, sir. My mother made it. I need to take it to the market."

The man brushed his fingers across the girl's face. "You could be quite pretty if you cleaned your face." He tore the front of the girl's dress. The girl cried out and begged him to stop. A shadow moved past the hole through which Madeline was looking.

It was Arik.

He snatched the officer away from the girl and slammed his face into the wall.

"Go!" Arik said.

The girl didn't wait for a second invitation. She hurried out of the room.

Madeline entered. "Don't. You promised me." She wasn't sure using his name in front of this man was wise.

"Do you know who I am?" the officer said.

Arik lifted his face from the wall and slammed it forward again, breaking his nose. "Yes, you're the broken-nosed officer!"

"I know people in high places. You don't want to hurt me."

"No, I don't. I want to kill you." He slammed the man's face into the wall again. Broken teeth fell to the floor.

"Cry and I will cut your tongue out and feed it to the dogs."

"What do you want from me?"

Madeline wanted to pull Arik off of the officer, but she didn't know what the man would do or what weapon he might have. If Arik was harmed in this time period, what would happen? She knew they shouldn't do anything to change the future. But could they die here? And what would be the consequences if they did? She moved in front of Arik so he could see her and shook her head. "You *promised* me! There will be consequences for this. Please let him go!"

Arik released the man. "Take the gold coins out," Arik said.

"Oh, so you want the gold, sir. Of course. Here they are. I have plenty."

He pulled his pouch out and poured the contents on the table. Gold coins dropped onto the wooden table, shining as if haunted by the spirits of the millions of lives lost because of them.

Arik's eyes were bloodshot. She could see his rage intensifying. She knew he would soon butcher this man. For some very unfortunate reason, she was able to read his mind now—she couldn't do it before. In his mind were terrifying images of cities falling because of the destruction of the plague. Dead bodies were piled up in front of houses on the street.

The Black Death spared no one—the rich, the poor, men, women, the old, the young. All perished. All because of the greed of this one man.

Before the man withdrew his hand from the coins, Arik swung the knife he had grabbed from the bench outside. The man's hand dropped to the table.

28

*D*inah liked her instantly. Jenny Bonneville was tall, fit, and agile judging by the way she walked. She had dark blonde hair and a quietly attractive face with eyes that told people she tolerated no bullshit. Her eyes zeroed in on Ciaran as they approached the line of cars and security. Ciaran stepped forward and embraced her. They were apparently closer acquaintances than Dinah had thought.

When they finished the hug of greeting, Jenny gestured at the security. "This is overkill, Ciaran," she said.

Ciaran smiled. "I know you're a capable woman, but I had already hired them. Might as well use them."

Jenny grinned. They went through the usual round of meet and greet, the sort of formal etiquette Dinah disliked anywhere in the multiverse. Her instincts usually told her whether she should like a person or not. Cooper was the same way. He had good instincts and — When she turned around, she was astonished to see her partner mesmerized by the sight of Jenny.

He had a girlfriend for pity's sake, and even though she was only into him for his abs—just a part of him, fake anyway, and definitely not his best asset—he wasn't exactly available.

"Cooper!"

"Huh?"

"Drooling in front of a girl doesn't give a good first impression."

"I wasn't staring!" He paused. "Was I?"

"Yes."

Ciaran approached with Jenny. "Jenny wants to go to Arik's place. I need to wait here for Madeline."

"I'll go with her," Cooper said quickly.

Ciaran raised an eyebrow.

"Cooper might be able to pick up some trails there that we can use. I'll go with them, too," Dinah added.

Ciaran nodded. "All right. Be careful."

Ciaran gave instructions to his security team. In no time, they were on their way to Arik's place.

DIANA WALKED out to the street and was greeted by the glorious sunshine of a beautiful day. She scoped out her surroundings. She wasn't sure where she was exactly. But she knew she was no longer in New York. Charming houses along small cobblestone streets welcomed her but made her feel like a tourist.

She couldn't ask people where she was because doing so would make her appear to be an old woman with dementia, so locating the local post office seemed to be a good way to determine her location. She went into a shop to ask for directions. Once she found the building, a sign there confirmed her suspicion that she was in England. Not only was she in England, she was in Oxford City.

She didn't need to be highly intelligent to predict she was close to where Arik lived. His address was in her pocket as she had been on her way to the post office in New York to send the package to him. They had snatched her when she'd turned the corner at the parking garage. She studied the tourist map she had picked up at the post office. Comparing it to the notes a very helpful officer had given her, she knew she was heading in the right direction to Arik's house.

The cold winter air couldn't chill the warm and cozy feel of the cottages along the pretty cobblestone street. She just knew there were stone fireplaces inside those cottages and families gathering together for a hot breakfast or scones and tea. She understood now why her son had fallen in love with the place. She'd rather he'd fall in love with his girlfriend more and make her a proud grandma, she thought.

Speaking of girlfriends, there was Grace standing directly in front of a cottage, which she guessed was Arik's house. She had met Grace a few times and had talked to her several times on the phone. She knew Arik's every movement thanks to Grace's reports, and she was very fond of this girl.

Grace was surprised to see Diana approaching. She rushed over to Diana. "Arik...he disappeared. He's gone. I've been waiting here for two days," Grace cried. Her face was a mess, her hair was tangled, and her eyes were hollow. She really did look as if she had been here for two days.

"It's okay, Grace. I want you to calm down and tell me what's going on. When did Arik disappear, and exactly what do you mean by that?"

"He told me to wait here for him. He went with that Irish girl to the market. He said he'd come back and have lunch with me, but he never did. I called him, but he didn't answer his phone." She was crying and talking at the same time, and Diana found it hard to understand her.

"Have you called the police?"

"No. Why would I do that? Arik told me to wait here."

Diana frowned. Something was wrong with this girl, she thought. Their encounters had always been brief. But now it dawned on her that had any of their interactions lasted longer, she would have seen that Grace was the perfect girlfriend—perfect looks, perfect speech, perfect behavior—but she functioned like a robot.

"All right, listen to me, Grace..." Her voice trailed off as she saw shadows creeping out from the darkness at the end of the dead-end street. After the encounter with her kidnapper, it was too quick to

jump to the conclusion that the what she saw approaching were actually *men*. But they moved like men, so she would try to deal with
them as such. It looked as if there were four of five of them. She
should have no problem handling them.

She shoved the package at Grace. "Can you hold this and stay
behind the fence?"

As she predicted, Grace took her order instantly without question. She grabbed the package and stepped behind the fence. Diana
picked up a stick that had been used to support a climbing plant from
the nearby garden and waited for the group of men to approach.

When they emerged from the dark corner, she saw it wasn't a
group of five. There were a dozen menacing men approaching her.

29

*C*iaran went back inside when he saw the group heading toward Arik's place. As soon as he entered the yard, he heard some noise at the back of the house. He rushed around the corner to find Madeline and Arik lying in the soil of the garden bed. He had known they would come back and Madeline would be fine but was still deliriously happy to see his prediction confirmed. He hurried over and saw Madeline's big brown eyes looking up at him from the ground.

He crouched, cupped her face, and rubbed his thumb on the dimple in her left cheek. "Which part of 'do not touch him' didn't you understand, First Councillor?"

"How can I resist a man that hot?"

He smiled, pulling her up, and kissed her. "I meant Arik," he said when their lips finally parted.

"I know." He kissed her again, stopping only when Arik opened his eyes groggily and sat up. Ciaran could see now what Arik meant when he said he was disoriented and totally confused whenever he returned from a time travel trip. Arik looked at Madeline, then at

Ciaran. Then he looked down at his hands, trying to remember and trying to understand the lingering sensations in his body.

Ciaran helped Madeline stand up and brushed the soil, leaves, and rose petals out of her hair. He wasn't sure of Arik's mental state, so he said nothing to him.

Arik looked at his hands again. Finding a couple of bruises and a faint trace of blood, he frowned. He looked at Madeline and asked, "You were with me? You traveled with me?"

"Huh?" Madeline blinked and acted confused, but Ciaran knew she was pretending. Putting on a poker face wasn't her strong suit, but she was lying for a reason.

"What's the last thing you remember?" Ciaran asked.

"We were at the market, and you shot at Dinah's friend."

Ciaran nodded. "Okay. That's not too bad. You only lost a few days."

"What?" Arik stood up and started pacing. "I've lost time. Okay... the market. What happened before that?" He continued to pace, asking himself questions.

Ciaran mouthed a question to Madeline. "Do you remember?"

She nodded. Then she projected her words into his mind as she had done many times before. *I can read his mind. Not now, but before and during the travel.*

Ciaran nodded. "Did he kill?" he mouthed.

Madeline shook her head.

"Mother!" Arik said the word as he remembered what happened at the market. "I have to get to the airport." He darted toward the gate.

Ciaran grabbed him. "You've tried a couple of times. There's no need to go now. Jenny has arrived. I sent others to go with her to your place."

"My place?"

"Yes, and—" Ciaran was interrupted when his wrist unit beeped. He glanced at the report. "Diana is here, too. Spotted in the city. We need to confirm it's her. The signal suggests she's heading toward your place as well, Arik," he said quickly and then strode to the car. Madeline and Arik followed.

AT ARIK'S PLACE, Diana tightened her grip on the garden stake, struck a ready position, and waited for the attackers coming toward her. She wondered if they would use guns. If they did, it would be the end of her. She decided she couldn't just stand there and wait. She needed to be more offensive and try to lure them away from Grace. She wasn't sure it was possible with a group of twelve men, but she had to try.

She heard a car brake and then footsteps coming up from behind her.

"Mom!" Jenny called.

She turned around and saw her daughter, a tall man, a tiny angelic girl, and a dozen security officers, armed to the teeth. The menacing men stopped in their tracks when they saw the new arrivals.

"Are you okay, Mom?"

"Yes. Why are you here?"

"Ciaran sent for me. He said some people might be after Arik."

Diana smiled and pointed her chin at the group that had stalled in the middle of the road. "They must be the ones after your brother."

"They're receiving instructions," Dinah said.

"Yes. They're mercenaries, and they're not from here. I mean, not from this dimension," Cooper added.

"What?" Jenny asked.

Before Cooper could answer, the men pulled their guns.

"Get down!" the head of security shouted from behind them.

Everyone dropped flat to the ground, leaving the two groups of fighters pointing guns at each other. Grace stepped out from behind the fence before anyone could shoot. She walked right between the two armed groups of men, shaking like a paper doll in a strong wind and clutching the package to her chest.

"Did you see Arik?" she asked as tears rolled down her face.

"Get down for God's sake!" Dinah shouted.

Grace kept walking as if in a deep trance. "Has anyone seen Arik?"

"Grace, get down on the ground," Diana commanded. But her command didn't work this time.

"He hasn't been home for days..."

The attackers lowered their guns and charged.

"They're going for the package! Do not shoot at the package. Use knives." Cooper shouted. They all jumped to their feet. The security officers had no choice but to lower their guns as well. They ran at the attackers. As Diana had predicted, the attackers were not human. As soon as they were killed by the security officers, they melted down into worm puddles.

In the haze and chaos of the fight, amid the screams and grunting and confusion, Diana looked back to find Grace.

"They've got her!" Diana shouted.

At the far end of the street, they saw a fighter running away. Grace hung over his shoulder, and the package was in his opposite hand. Before he reached the corner that turned onto a larger road, he vanished, along with Grace and the package.

As soon as that happened, the remaining mercenaries turned, ran in the same direction, and disappeared.

"How can they just disappear like that?" Jenny asked incredulously.

"They didn't. They jumped into a dimensional gate," Cooper said.

Behind them, a car fishtailed and stopped right in the middle of the road. Arik stormed out. He said nothing but rushed toward his mother, embracing her.

Diana could feel every ounce of muscle in her son's body quivering. At that moment, she understood that, regardless of the reason he'd put the barrier between them for years, she had never lost him. He was still her beloved and caring son.

Then out of the car stepped her second son, Ciaran, and a beautiful woman. She didn't need an introduction to know that this was Ciaran's woman.

30

*H*e put the package on the table and lay an unconscious Grace on the floor. Her dead weight was heavier than he thought. He readied the heavy-duty, multiversal, military-grade gun in his pocket. He was pleased he had gotten what he needed today without having to discharge his precious weapon. He was even more pleased thinking about the credits he was going to get for this job. He could choose to receive Earth money, the easiest form of currency to launder in the multiverse, but he preferred multiversal credits. That way, he could use them in any universe he chose to live in. The only downside was that he had to legitimize the credits before he could use them. This was a task many wouldn't voluntarily choose. But he liked challenges.

On the floor, Grace's eyes fluttered. "Shit," he muttered to himself. He didn't want her to wake this early and see him. He hadn't tied her up, thinking the drug would have a more lasting effect on her. He didn't like lingering relationship with a client, let alone, a merchandise. When he handed her over to his client, she would no longer be his problem, awake or not.

She closed her eyes again. "Great!" He exhaled, feeling relief. But then he didn't like the idea of a woman unconscious and tied up in the hands of a faceless man. He shook his head, telling himself this was only another job.

He shouldn't call his client faceless, but he really was faceless on all counts. He'd never met him, never seen a picture, and never had a direct conversation. If that wasn't faceless, what was?

The screen on the wall flashed and turned on. On it was the image of an odd flower—his client's symbol. He referred to himself as Arete. He couldn't care less what the symbol or the name meant because whatever it was, it was fake. *Who cares?* he thought.

The voice had been filtered via the robotic signal system. Even so, he could still tell it was the voice of a male creature from Xiilok. He adopted his poker face and listened with respect. Any creature who wanted to pay him was his friend.

The voice asked, "Do you have the merchandise, DT5?"

The client referred to him by the job ID. "Yes." He pushed the package forward on the table.

"What is that rag on the floor?"

"You wanted the package and the recipient. That's the recipient. And she's a *person,* not a rag."

"No, it is not."

"Excuse me?"

"That's beside the point. Regarding the job, you have not fulfilled your contract. I can't pay you. The agreement was that you get me the package and its intended recipient."

"That wasn't specified in the contract."

"Are you stupid? There's no need to specify that trivial matter. Any package is intended for someone. Why would I want a random creature who was carrying my precious package?"

"That's not my problem. The job is delivered. I want my money."

"I won't pay for a half-finished job."

He nodded. "All right." He grabbed the package.

"Fine," Arete said. "I'll pay for the package only. Leave it. You won't get my business in the future."

He shrugged. He wouldn't want to do business with this client again anyway.

A small window on the wall slid open, and a keyboard came out from inside the wall. "Type in where you want the money sent."

He nodded and approached the keyboard. As soon as he pressed the first key, a stream of fumes exploded from underneath the keyboard. It was intended to blast straight into his face, but years of training in one of the best combat hubs in the cosmos had served him well. This little stunt wouldn't kill him.

He jumped aside, tripped on Grace's legs, and fell to the floor. The toxic fumes spread quickly. He was dazed, but he had gotten past the first blast and knew he could survive this. On the floor, he could see that the woman he'd captured was unconscious. If he fled right now, she would definitely be dead.

He didn't know when he had grown sentimental, but he scrambled up to his feet, threw Grace over his shoulders, and darted out of the room.

31

S tanding on the road in front of his house, Arik was totally confused. His mother and sister were there, but now they had Grace and the package. What did they want from him? Arik saw the yellow-eyed man again, standing at the far end of the bridge. He wasn't sure if the others could see him, but he no longer cared. He needed answers. From the look on Ciaran's face, he had seen the man, too. Without a word, the two darted toward the bridge.

They caught up with the man quickly when he turned a corner, ran behind a church, and entered the church cemetery. The yellow-eyed man stopped and waited.

Before he could utter a word, Ciaran said, "We don't have time to play your cryptic game. Last time, you said you wanted me to convince Arik to help you. Now that he's here, you can talk to him about whatever you want. But first things first—you have to help us."

The man smiled. "The legendary Ciaran LeBlanc, always wheeling and dealing for the multiverse. I am happy to be at your service."

"Do the packages being delivered all over the multiverse have anything to do with Xiilok rebels?" Ciaran asked.

"I can't speak for others. I only know these packages are not from my camp. We are peaceful."

Arik snorted. "He wanted me to help his camp liberate Xiilok, the land of the multiversal outlaws, and he hopes to do that by peaceful protests!"

Ciaran shook his head. "You can't control Xiilok with peace."

The man nodded. "I know, and I have learned my lesson. I'm here to release you from your duties to us, Arik."

"What? Why now?"

"I am only the leader of a small branch in a camp. We operate by the light, as you might know, Arik." He looked at Ciaran. "Our light is like energy in your universe." Ciaran nodded, and the yellow-eyed man continued. "We owed the Red Eye's tribe, and they have traded us."

"For whom?" Ciaran asked.

"I don't know. Maybe the Black Rock and other satellite universes from Xiilok, those that need labor."

"By labor, do you mean slavery?" Arik asked.

"I don't have a choice. I have already given my gift to you, Arik. If I can't take care of my people, I have to let them go. I have only a day left."

"What about Xanthe?" Arik asked.

The man looked at Ciaran. "Xanthe is our healer. She took care of him when he was injured." He looked back at Arik. "Xanthe herself should be fine. She has skills. They wouldn't use her as a slave. I can't guarantee anything for her family, though."

"But they're women and children. They're trainees. They will have skills in the future!" Arik exclaimed.

The yellow-eyed man raised an eyebrow. "I am a poor leader. I can't negotiate that for them. It is very likely the Xanthe family will be traded to the Black Rock, where medical skills are needed most."

"Nobody can treat the Black Rock. They're the cancer of the multiverse. They should be killed," Arik snarled.

Ciaran smiled. "I agree. You know about the multiverse more than I'd expect, Arik."

"I'm afraid you're not in a position to say that, Arik. Our problem is not your concern anymore," the man said.

"Since when?"

"Well, since now. I am here to release you from your position."

"But you said your gift, once given, can't be taken back."

"That is right. But the position of leader is not a gift. It's an honor from the tribe and a responsibility—one you didn't want to take." The man nodded his goodbye. "That is all for now." He turned to leave.

Arik said, "If I take the position, I won't liberate Xiilok, even with peaceful protests. If that neck of the cosmos woods is uninhabitable, I'll move my people elsewhere."

"What does that mean?"

"I won't put women and children at war, even if it's a defensive war. Even if they call me a wussified piece of wet toast."

The man frowned. "Is that a promise?"

"Only if you leave all the trainees out of the fight."

The man sighed. "All right." He approached and reached out his hand for a handshake.

"Are you sure, Arik?" Ciaran asked. "It doesn't appear that you can take back whatever it is you're about to agree to."

"Do I have a choice?" Arik asked and clasped the man's hand. At the point of contact, he grunted. A light was exchanged between them, and their bodies glowed. After a moment, they let go of each other's hands. The yellow-eyed man looked as if he had aged ten years in that brief moment. Arik's skin glowed with a shade of yellow light which soon dissipated.

"You're now the leader of the Yellow Shield tribe, the Third Circle, Xiilok, effective tomorrow."

Arik squared his shoulders in an attempt to rid himself of the tingling sensation. He said nothing.

The man turned toward Ciaran. "I'll get more men and merge with the Sixth Circle as you suggested. If I could get the ex-Eudaizians to join, they would be the majority of the tribe, and we could be under your protection. Do I have your word?"

"What?" Arik exclaimed.

"I'm trying to get us under the protection of a Eudaizian troop. This collaboration is the last good thing I can do for the tribe."

"What the hell? Will I be consulted on this?" Arik asked and pointed at Ciaran. "He's violent! He pro-war!"

Ciaran raised an eyebrow. "I don't think you know me that well, Arik." He turned toward the man. "Yes, you have my word."

"Thank you for your help. Now we have both a leader and protection from your troops. We have never done this well for so long. It is worth the sacrifice. Thank you again!"

Ciaran reached out his hand to shake. "It's my pleasure. You're a brave man."

"What the fuck does that mean?" Arik asked.

The yellow-eyed man nodded a goodbye to Ciaran and smiled at Arik. "I have things to take care of. If I die before tomorrow, you might have to start a day earlier." He turned and then vanished through a dimensional gateway.

Arik was about to shove Ciaran's shoulder, but Ciaran raised a finger to stop him. "I don't care for being pushed. So don't do it, Arik."

"Did you plot all this?"

"Not at all. But the man needed my help, didn't he?" Ciaran shrugged and walked away.

32

*W*hen Arik and Ciaran came back to the house, Arik thought the air felt heavy as lead. His mother and sister looked at him, saying nothing.

Arik turned to Jenny. "All right, it looks as though there's something you think you should tell me, but you won't because it will put me in danger," Arik said.

Nobody spoke.

"If this is about Grace, I need to know."

Silence.

"Oh come on, he has the right to know!" Dinah exclaimed.

Arik zeroed in on Dinah. "Please, Dinah. Whatever it is, I can take it."

"We got a message asking you to meet them or they'll kill Grace."

"Who..." Arik and Ciaran asked at the same time. Ciaran stopped, gesturing Arik to go ahead with the question.

"Who are they, and when and where do I meet them?"

"We've been asking the same questions," Cooper said.

"How did they leave the message?" Ciaran asked.

Cooper showed Ciaran the picture he had taken on his wrist unit

—a puff of purple powder stuck on a door with the etched words, *Meet now, or she will die.*

"We heard a thunk at the door. After Dinah confirmed the power wasn't toxic, I took the picture, and the text vanished."

Jenny pointed. "Your nose is bleeding, Arik."

Arik wiped the blood away and winced at his pounding headache. The lyrics and beats of "Crossroads" echoed in his mind again. He sat down and grabbed his head. If he wasn't careful, he might heat up and begin to time travel at this critical point. Maybe he shouldn't think right now. He'd wait until it passed.

"He hears 'Crossroads' in his head, Ciaran. Does that mean anything to you?" Madeline asked.

Ciaran paced around the room, then back and forth. He turned his wrist unit on to do some research then gave up the idea. There wouldn't be enough time. "Is there anything nearby—a church, a temple, or another place of worship—that's called Crossroads, Arik?" Ciaran asked.

Arik shook his head, which was still buried in his hands.

"Cooper, can I have a list of those places, please?" Ciaran asked.

"You got it," Cooper said and dove into the task using his wrist unit. In about ten seconds, he said, "I've got a full list of churches, temples, places of worship, and anything else that only the god of the multiverse knows the purpose of."

Ciaran pointed his wrist unit toward Cooper. There was a quick flash. "Thank you," Ciaran said.

Cooper stared down at his wrist unit and mumbled, "Did he just cop the data out of my unit? I have a passcode."

Dinah chuckled. "That's called scanning, Cooper. And your pass-code is your last name and your birthday. Everyone in the cosmos knows that secret! The only thing Ciaran can't scan is your mind." Then she looked at Madeline. "Without the help of his walking talking mind scanner, that is."

"They're at Carfax Tower," Ciaran said.

Arik's head popped up from his hands. "Carfax means crossroads.

Why the heck didn't I think of that?" Ciaran and Arik charged out the door.

Everyone followed, but Cooper lingered behind, glancing at the door where the message had been left before.

"Cooper, aren't you coming with us?" Dinah called.

"Yes, but give me a moment."

Dinah returned to him. "What's wrong with the door?"

"The message didn't specifically mention Arik or Grace, or the place to meet." He turned toward Dinah. "I think they don't know. I think they're as confused as we are, and they're probably relying on us to get the clues."

"You're right...and..." Dinah trailed off, pulling Cooper behind the door with her.

Across the road, a man strode quickly along, trailing the group heading toward the Carfax Tower. "There's our tail," Cooper said.

Dinah waited until the man walked beyond the door where they were hiding then stepped out and pumped a sedative needle. He turned around to see what had happened, but it took only two seconds for the sedative to work. He flopped to the ground.

"All right, you go. I'll take care of this," Cooper said and darted over to pull the man into the yard. Dinah hurried in the direction the group had just gone.

33

*R*unning along the road, Arik and Ciaran heard a sound like someone had dropped a sack of potatoes on the ground. They both looked to one side of them then the other. There were no potatoes, but on a brick wall, there was a large circle of purple powder on the wall that looked exactly like the picture Cooper had shown them. Text appeared like someone was writing in the powder. *Meet at Crossroads, Arik.*

"Didn't we just see this message?" Arik said.

"Yes, except the location and your name weren't mentioned in the other one," Ciaran said.

"Is it a trap?" Arik asked.

Ciaran shook his head. "No, I think whoever is playing this head game with us is solving the puzzle, one step at a time. They might keep pace with us, or they might even be a step ahead, but I think someone or something is still figuring out something that we might have the answers to."

"But we don't even know the questions!" Arik exclaimed.

"We do. We need to know what you have to do with this. I think you hold the key to this multiverse killing frenzy. You have to figure this out—both the questions and the answers."

"So let's go," Arik muttered and strode ahead.

Carfax Tower, an imposing tower that provided the highest vantage point of Oxford City, was located at the center of the city.

"It's a tourist attraction," Diana said with a sigh.

"A disaster attraction," Madeline said.

They closed the distance and could see the tower clearer. It was a square thirteenth-century stone tower. The majority of the church that had existed around it had been destroyed, leaving it standing isolated and alone. There was one small door that served as the entrance, where tourists purchased tickets and then headed up several sets of stone stairs which led to the top of the tower.

The only exit was at the top. Tourists exited the staircase one person at a time and followed a narrow stone-railed balcony that wrapped around the tower roof. There, the one-way lane of tourists could look out over the city. They then had to loop around and exit the roof via the same door, heading down the stairs this time.

At the corner of the roof, there was a light flash—once, twice, and then a third time. At the third flash, a creature of human size and shape with a lizard-like head stood up. Grace was held captive by the sight of it. Her hair was tangled, her face soaked with tears, her eyes filled with fear. She clutched the package to her chest.

A line of three tourists had made it out to the rooftop. The creature pointed a gun at the man in the front and fired. The two women standing behind the man screamed and retreated back through the doorway. The dead man toppled over the stone rail of the balcony and fell to the ground.

People on the ground screamed. A swarm of men and women flowed out from inside the tower onto the street.

Arik hurried toward the entrance.

Jenny and Diana followed, but Ciaran pulled them back. "Look at the tower. It's going to be small and confined inside. You'll only block his way coming out."

"You expect us to stand here and watch?" Jenny said.

Madeline wrapped her arms around the two women to hold them back and clear the way for Ciaran. "At critical times like this, listening to Ciaran is always the best option. Trust me. You'll thank me later," Madeline said.

Ciaran left the women, rushed toward Arik, and grabbed his elbow as he made his way through the stream of panicked tourists pouring out from the tower. "I can take that creature from the ground. You just need to buy me some time. But shooting from such a distance in these chaotic conditions might not turn out the way we want. Whatever the result is, I need you to remember that you're now the leader of the Yellow Shield tribe in Xiilok. Every decision you make—including your life and death—has consequences and affects many others. You don't have to be a hero, but don't be an idiot."

"Understood." Arik shrugged off Ciaran's hand.

"No, I don't think you understand. Let me sum it up for you—if you have to choose between your life and another's, you have to protect your own. Your life is important to a lot of people."

"I agree," Dinah said.

She was so tiny they hadn't noticed that she had been keeping pace at Arik's side the whole time.

"Are you going to give me a gun to protect myself?" Arik asked.

"No. With that narrow balcony, you can only go head on, and you'll lose to the space creature."

"Thanks for the fucking vote of confidence."

"Dinah will have a gun, but she'll be behind you." Ciaran pulled out one of his guns and handed it to her. "This is a real gun, Dinah—"

"Yes, it can shoot nine simultaneous beams at ninety-one angles and automatically recharge at ninety percent of ammunition and with optional insertion of natural energy."

Ciaran smiled.

Dinah grinned. "I don't have access, but that doesn't mean I don't know Eudaizian guns." She winked at him then made some adjustments to the gun and tucked it inside her jacket. Arik rolled his eyes.

As Dinah and Arik entered the tower, Ciaran went back to Diana,

Jenny, and Madeline. He looked into Diana's eyes. "I'll shoot at the creature when Arik gets up there. I'm a very good shot, but—"

She placed a finger to his lips to stop him from talking. "Do what you have to do, son."

Ciaran nodded and moved toward the tower.

34

The staircase inside the tower was extremely steep and narrow. It could only accommodate one-way traffic for average-sized people. While Dinah had no trouble, Arik almost hit his head against the stone arches a few times. At the top of the staircase, they exited through a tiny door and stepped out onto the balcony. It was bright, cold, and windy. Upon walking through the doorway, Arik could see the creature and Grace standing to his right at the very end of the narrow balcony.

He glanced down to the ground and saw a crowd of people looking up to the rooftop in panic. They had called the police, he figured, but earthly law enforcement would be too late and too slow for this. Plus, he didn't think combating space creatures would have been something covered in the standard police training manual.

Ciaran prowled among the people on the ground like a hungry leopard. Arik knew he was looking for one clear shot to take the creature down without killing Grace. But Arik knew Ciaran well enough —if push came to shove, he would take down both the creature and Grace if they posed any danger to Arik.

That was Ciaran's philosophy and what he had been talking

about before Arik had climbed the stairs of the tower. He took pity on Ciaran sometimes. He'd had some heavy duties heaped on his shoulders at a very young age and was always on important missions. There was always the bigger picture in Ciaran's life. Important matters to consider. Hard decisions to make. Well, he knew the time had come for him to do what Ciaran did, and that time was beginning now.

Grace was shaking in the wind.

"I'm here. I guess you want to see me," Arik said to the creature. "I speak English, and I know only two French words well—yes and no. Other than that, I'm afraid you'll have to use body language."

"Come here!" the creature croaked.

"It's too narrow for me to go over there. We'll kind of lump together in that corner, and I'm really not in the mood for romance. So why don't you let Grace come over here, and then I'll head over to your side. She's skinny. She can squeeze past me."

"Come here," the creature croaked again.

"Right, so your English is equivalent to my French." Arik moved a fraction of an inch forward. From the corner of his eye, he could see that Ciaran had stopped his movement on the ground. He was losing his patience. He wouldn't take a chance of the creature shooting at Arik.

Arik said to Grace, "Honey, you're going to be okay."

She nodded.

He needed her to nod harder or do something to move her head away from the lizard's.

"Is the package heavy? Why don't you put it down, or maybe give it to me?" He inched another step forward, reaching his hands out as if to take the package. Grace bent over a bit, trying to give it to him. The creature yanked her back.

"Come closer!" the creature growled. It bared its teeth and poked one sharp fang into Grace's neck. A small stream of blood seeped out.

"Okay, I'll come closer." He inched forward another step.

Arik felt a movement at his back. Dinah had ducked to the

ground and pumped a needle out from between his legs, hitting Grace's leg.

"Ouch!" Grace yelped and bent down to see what had hit her. As soon as her head moved away from the lizard, Ciaran fired a precise laser beam at its head. The lizard's head was sheared off, and it exploded in midair. Its body slid down to the ground and in a flash melted into a puddle of worms.

"That was a damn good shot," Arik said.

Grace stood up, mesmerized for a moment by the lizard's brain matter raining down on her. Then she screamed.

"Will your needle put her to sleep? She'll topple over the rail!" Arik said with concern.

"No, it was a placebo," Dinah said.

Arik chuckled and turned toward Grace, who was still crying. "It's okay, honey. We'll clean you up," he said as he approached her.

On the ground, Cooper charged toward Diana, Jenny, Madeline, and Ciaran, waving his hand frantically in the air and pointing at the tower.

From the tower, Dinah frowned at the scene below and engaged her wrist unit to Cooper's. She looked at the screen. *Signal jammed*, it said.

"Cooper!" Dinah called out loud, but the distance was too far for her voice to travel. Arik turned and looked at her.

"What is it, Dinah?"

"I'm trying to call Cooper. But the signal jammed," Dinah said. As Arik was looking at her, Dinah could see the expression on Grace's face had changed.

"Let's get down to the ground, Arik," Dinah said and withdrew toward the door, which was located just a few steps behind her.

Arik shrugged. "Sure, wasn't that the plan?" He turned to look at Grace, who now had a smile on her face.

Dinah gazed through the crowd and saw Cooper frantically explaining something to the group. She looked back at her wrist unit. The signal was still jammed.

35

"*A*re you sure?" Ciaran asked.

Cooper paced back and forth. "More than sure. Someone is jamming all the signals. I've tried to call her. I am one thousand percent sure that the guy got the real Grace. I know it was a small window in the back of the car, but trust me, that stunning woman was the real Grace. The thing up in the tower with Arik and Dinah is not."

Ciaran tried his unit again. It was too late to run back to the tower to take care of the fake Grace. Arik was already standing next to her and was about to embrace her.

"What does it want?" asked Ciaran.

He saw Arik turn and look at him. He immediately waved his hand, gesturing him to get away from Grace. But Grace also saw the signal. She turned and looked at Arik.

Madeline concentrated. She had peeked into Dinah's mind before. She could do it again. She channeled a message to her. *Grace is a Xiilok creature.*

Grace reached out, trying to grab Arik's shirt and pull him back to her. Dinah pulled out her gun, but Arik was blocking her shot.

Arik pushed Grace away. Dinah ducked again but still couldn't find a clear angle to shoot. The balcony was too narrow for Arik or her to do anything.

"Back out, Arik," she said. She backed up and stood right in the doorway. Grace grabbed Arik. He pushed her away to free himself, and she dropped the package to the floor of the balcony so that she could grab him with both hands. Arik shoved her harder. Metal nails erupted through Grace's fingertips and punctured his shoulders.

"Ouch," he grunted.

"She's fake! Throw her over the balcony, Arik!" Dinah shouted.

"What?"

While he was distracted, Grace slashed at his chest. Her long nails had grown out like blades. Arik wouldn't throw a woman over the balcony. Dinah knew that. Even if he wanted to, Grace now had ten menacing nail blades that could slice through an artery in a second.

Grace's eyes became bloodshot, and she stopped holding Arik.

"Oh no," Dinah muttered.

It was too late for Arik to do anything.

Dinah leaped to the outside of the balcony, grabbing the rail with one hand. Dangling from the balcony of the tower, she now had a clear shot at Grace. Without hesitation, she pulled the gun Ciaran had given her and savaged that pretty head in one shot. Like the lizard's, the head exploded. But unlike the lizard, the body didn't instantly disintegrate into a puddle of worms. Instead, it stabbed its nails through the package, puncturing it with ten holes. Arik kicked the body. It tumbled over the rail and dropped to the ground below.

The holes in the package taunted him. This was how jumpers got killed. Dinah had told him they had been exposed to packages. The packages killed indiscriminately—both jumpers and ordinary people. But this package was meant for him.

Specifically.

The time travel had sent him everywhere. The songs had been sent to his head to drive him crazy and heat up his body, triggering the travel. Each time he traveled, a certain set of songs kept playing in his head, and it had nothing to do with his musical preferences as he had previously thought.

It was the frequency they were after.

Something or someone was tuning him like one tuned a radio.

And this package might be the last station.

It was too late. He couldn't run away from it now. He could see the holes opening wider.

He couldn't throw the package into the crowd below.

He had to get away from it. That way, they would miss their tuning station. It would be just a puff of powder on the dirty rooftop of an old building.

But there was only one way out of this. One way down.

Arik stood up.

He heard screams echoing up from the crowd below as if they knew his intention.

It was a long distance away, but he thought he saw his mother's eyes looking up at him. She didn't cry but looked at him with support. His mother always supported his decisions, no matter what they were.

He gazed in his mother's direction a few seconds longer, then hurtled over the rail and freefell.

36

*D*angling from the balcony, Dinah saw Arik leap over the rail and freefall from the roof of Carfax Tower. So much for Ciaran's speech about how Arik should put a high value on his life. Dinah sighed, let go of the rail, and fell after him. She hoped the wings Ciaran had made for her worked.

When she had closed the distance with Arik, she flipped out her wings. The two gigantic and magnificent wings on her back spread out. She grabbed Arik before he hit the ground. He wrapped his arms around her waist. She flapped the wings, and they took off just before their bodies scraped the ground.

She flapped her wings once more, and they sailed off, carried by the wind. She had never loved winter breezes that much, but it now felt as if an ocean of cool energy was flowing into her body. She inhaled the fresh air, savored the warmth of Arik's arms around her waist and the feel of his body pressed against hers.

She flapped once more, and they flew higher. She wanted it to last forever. She couldn't remember the last time she had experienced such freedom.

She grinned down at Arik. "Go for a ride?" She didn't need an answer from him. Nobody in his right mind would say no to flying.

She flapped again and again.

"Thank you for saving me," Arik said.

"Well, it's only because you haven't yet given me the answers I'm looking for about the apertures."

"I'll give them to you when we get down."

"I'm sorry about Grace. I mean, not the fake one. The real one. But Cooper and I will find her for you."

Arik sighed. "You don't need to find her. She doesn't belong to this world."

"I know. She seems perfectly unreal."

Arik shook his head. "I meant that the human Grace died five years ago. What you see now is a version of her. Like a projection of her ideal person, if that makes any sense."

"I thought only Eudaiz had the technology to make a live, interactive profile."

"Grace's case isn't a robotic profile. It's the creation of a tribe in Xiilok. She wished for it. And she got her wish granted. It's a long story."

"I've got time."

They heard a tear and then felt the impact of a sudden stop. They had flown straight into a tree. Dinah's wings were caught among the tree branches. She tugged at her right wing. A thread at the edge of the wing broke, rolled back, and snapped at her wrist unit. It fell to the ground. She looked down, and the ground seemed quite a distance away. They were dangling from the top of a tree.

She tried to flap again, but the wings wouldn't move. Arik's arms were still wrapped around her waist, and his face rubbed against her breasts.

"Okay, you'll have to jump down from here, Arik."

"I can't. I'm afraid of heights."

"You just jumped out of the tallest tower in Oxford. This is only a low tree."

"I didn't have a choice before."

"And you don't have a choice now. My wrist unit is on the ground, and I'm stuck in the tree with you. We can't call for rescue unless you get that wrist unit."

"Why can't we both jump down? As you said, it's a low tree. Twisted ankles would be the worst case scenario, I'd guess."

"These wings are built into my one and only jacket. If I slide out of them, I'll be topless."

"I see… I mean, I understand. But I can't let you hang in the tree by yourself!"

"Oh no! No!" Dinah shouted down.

Arik looked down and saw a dog approaching the wrist unit on the ground. It sniffed at it. It might be his imagination, but this one looked a lot like the dog that had mistakenly accused him of carrying drugs at the French airport. But this dog was younger. It couldn't be the same one.

"That dog hates me. It's seeking revenge for his…his relative!" Arik said.

"What?"

Arik yelled down to the dog, "Hey, don't swallow that. It'll explode, and you'll be nothing but meat."

"You're talking to a dog, Arik."

"Yes, apparently. Someone has to, or it'll swallow the one and only device that people can use to track us."

"Just jump down and get it, will you?"

"I don't like dogs."

"Arik! You're afraid of heights, and you don't like dogs. Do you have any survival skills at all?"

"Yes, I understand Irish accents—or Iilos accents in your case. Does that count?"

"No!"

"Why not?"

"Not to you. To the dog. It ate my unit!"

37

*I*n front of the tower, the police had arrived. There were no traces of the creature. Even the worm puddles where their bodies had dissolved had already been absorbed into the soil. The police set up quarantine barricades around the tower in a flash. An expert biohazard team was sent up to the roof but had apparently found nothing but an empty box and traces of a powder made from garden flowers.

Ciaran and his people left the scene quickly before the police had a chance to question them. He didn't believe the earthly authorities would help in this case, nor did he believe he could help them.

Back at Arik's place, they looked around, but Arik and Dinah were nowhere to be found.

"All right, I don't know where they flew to. Dinah isn't answering her wrist unit, so I'll activate her rescue device," Ciaran said. He turned on the device, and in a few minutes, they heard signals.

"Dinah," Ciaran said.

"Oh, Ciaran! Yes, I can hear you. But I don't know where from."

"I just activated your rescue unit. It's in the top button of your jacket. Are you okay?"

"Yes."

Ciaran turned on the speaker so the others could hear. They heard a loud ruffling noise.

"Where are you?" Cooper asked.

"Top of the other hill. We're stuck in a tree... I can't find it... It flipped inside... Oh no, it's sliding down."

"I can see it," said Arik.

"I can feel it. Get your face out of my breasts so I can slide my hand in... Oops! No...no! It's going down... Ciaran, can you still hear me?"

"Yes."

"Your rescue unit dropped inside my jacket, Ciaran. It's sliding down... Hold on..." said Dinah.

"It slid in between her breasts and down," said Arik.

"Stop peeking," said Dinah.

"I'm not. They're right in my face," said Arik. "Stop wriggling, Dinah."

"I'm trying to get the unit. If it drops, the dog will get it, too."

"Ouch, you just kicked me," said Arik. "All right, I think we're going down now. Hold tight. Ouch, not there! That's my injured shoulder," said Arik.

Then they heard the loud noise of tearing fabric.

"Can I follow the signal to go rescue my partner?" Cooper asked.

"You certainly can," Ciaran said and gave Cooper the device.

"It sounds like my brother got tangled up in some breasts. I'll go along to rescue him, too," Jenny said.

Diana shrugged out of her jacket. "With that much torn fabric, I guess you might need something for the little angel with wings who saved my son. So take this with you."

COOPER CHECKED the map again and pointed to the top of the hill. "They're up there." Jenny nodded and followed. The path was blocked by a large rock. Cooper jumped on top of it and reached his hand down to help Jenny up. She paused to look at his hand then smiled and accepted his offer.

"So you and Dinah come from another place, huh?"

"You make it sound like we're from heaven or something. But we only come from another universe."

"So is it a different world then?"

Cooper shrugged. "I'm not the best person to ask these kinds of questions. But I think that once you get out to the multiverse, things become a lot easier. They just make sense. If you've lived on Earth and in this world the whole time, then it's hard to explain. I'm not saying which one is better. Sometimes it's better if you don't know jack."

Jenny smiled and said nothing.

"So you teach martial arts like Diana. That's very cool!"

She nodded. "I practice aikido. It's a kind of martial arts for defense."

"So you don't attack at all? Wouldn't it be better to just run fast?"

Jenny laughed. "What if you can't run?"

Cooper shrugged. "I guess you've got a point."

"What would you do if you were in danger and couldn't run, Cooper?"

"I'd apply Cooper's three-step rule. One, I'd talk my way out of it. Two, I'd *really* talk my way out of it. And three, I'd tell people I am talking my way out of the shit they're creating for me. And they really shouldn't want me to stop talking because outside the talking rules, I wouldn't be too polite."

Jenny smiled and said nothing. They headed up the hill, and in the distance, they could see Arik carrying Dinah down the hill.

Cooper rushed over and saw she was wearing Arik's jacket. "She twisted her ankle," Arik said.

38

*C*iaran took Madeline to the back garden. The last few days had been hectic, and there were times when he had almost lost her. He needed reassurance that they were now safe and sound and could go back to Eudaiz to see their children. He rubbed his thumb over the dimple in Madeline's left cheek. "Thank you," he said.

"For what?"

"For coming here with me." He smiled and kissed her.

"I'm glad I had the chance to meet your best friend and see the two of you make up for the lost time. Arik is a treasure."

He nodded.

"When we time traveled, Arik would've killed a man to stop the plague if I hadn't talked him out of it. And today, he would have given up his life to prevent a toxic explosion. He has a big heart, Ciaran."

"He's a good man. But he didn't jump to his death today, because if he had, he would have disappointed me a great deal."

"What?"

"We signed him up for a position at Xiilok before we came to the tower. Arik received a gift from a tribe in Xiilok. He's in possession of one of the most precious resources in the cosmos—the light. He hasn't received any training yet, but my understanding is that he could be as light as the light."

"What do you mean?"

"Simply speaking, he could turn his body into a chosen property of the light. I don't think he would let his body hit the ground like a sack of potatoes. "

"Do you think he knows his abilities?"

Ciaran nodded. "He knows the gift he received and the responsibility that comes with it. He just didn't want the responsibility before."

"So you let Dinah think he'd jump to his death to protect strangers. Ciaran, she tried to rescue him with her angel wings!"

Ciaran chuckled. "There's nothing wrong with believing in a fairy tale. As long as you don't overdo it, it's quite romantic, don't you think?"

She kissed his cheek. "Charming!" she said.

"To congratulate Arik on his new position, I've ordered a special gift for him. It's Stevie Ray Vaughan's original 1963 Number One Stratocaster."

"No, you didn't!" Madeline slapped Ciaran's chest lightly. "Really?"

He nodded. "Yes. He lost his precious guitar when we met. So I figured this replacement would be just the thing."

She smiled. "You're very sweet."

"That's to make up for the time I'm not sweet. It seems whatever I do, the bitter taste is always stronger."

The smile faded from Madeline's face. "Xiilok."

Ciaran whirled around. "Where?"

The walls in front of them flashed in a purple shade, and a distant, elderly male voice came out from the wall. "Greetings!" The image of a strange-looking flower appeared with the word *Arete* printed above it. The flower had the features of a rose, a lily, and a daisy combined.

Ciaran pulled his gun and pointed at the wall.

"Is this how Eudaizians greet people?" the voice said.

"You're a wall, not a person," Ciaran said.

"I've come to show my appreciation. I enjoyed the thrill today. I have been hunting everywhere. But after the today's exercise, I think I am getting close."

"Close to what? Who are you?" Ciaran asked.

"Arete."

"You're Xiilok rebels. What do you want from us?"

"What I want for Xiilok is the same as what you want for Eudaiz, Ciaran."

"I don't know who you are, but I doubt we share anything, including our view of the politics of the cosmos. Regarding your exercise today, you have no right to it, and it has cost innocent lives. You will have to pay for this."

"You worry me! You might not be a compatible game partner. That would be boring."

"This is no game."

"It is to me. And I don't think you have a choice. Your friend, Arik Bonneville, isn't as strong as you are, and he has no experience, but we value him. He gave us the perfect tune. If you leave him for us, I'll trade you two thousand ex-Eudaizians."

"If those Eudaizians left us to join you, you can keep them."

"Four thousand."

"I said keep them."

"All right. I just want to let you know I have engaged the game, and I've pushed out a few challenges to the multiversal game council."

"If it's a game, it won't have real consequences," Madeline said.

"It's not just any game. It's a multiversal hologame. Your husband should educate you about the game rules."

Ciaran blasted at the image on the wall.

"You disappoint me, Ciaran. Why would you shoot the messenger? I'm just a wall, right? Am I upsetting you that much?"

"Not at all. I'm capturing your message frequency and measuring the capability of your technology." He looked at his wrist unit then shook his head and shrugged. "All right. I'll take whatever challenge you can come up with."

"Our technology is much more advanced than yours, Ciaran."

"Whatever you say." He shrugged and looked bored. "Anything else you want to tell me?"

"I challenged the rebel tribe in Xiilok led by your dear friend, Arik. I also challenged a few leaders in Iilos. As for Eudaiz, I challenge you and your entire council."

"That's a very ambitious bet. What did you have to put in as a deposit? It's very long odds that you'd win."

Arete chuckled. "As you've said, it's a very ambitious bet. The resources I have are so impressive that the game council accepted my deposit. So you'll get the invitation soon. For your information, my bet is seven billion. That is all for now. Goodbye. I hope you like the flower I gave you, Madeline."

The image on the wall disappeared.

"What flower?" Ciaran asked.

Madeline shoved her hand into her jacket pocket and pulled out the purple flower the old peasant had given her in 1348 at Dorset. Arik had thrown it away, but she had picked it up again when he wasn't paying attention. She thought when they traveled back to the present time, the flower would be gone. But it wasn't.

"What's going on, Ciaran?" she asked.

"Seven billion is the Earth's population," he said.

She looked into his strikingly beautiful eyes. For the first time since she had known him, and after all the life and death battles they had been through, she saw the confidence in those eyes waver.

"Look out!" Ciaran shouted and pushed her to the ground.

There was a thunk, and a surge of purple powder flew against the wall in front of them. Text appeared. *Congratulations! You have passed the entry level of the multiversal hologame. You have been invited to the next level. Your opponents are waiting to defeat you.*

EPILOGUE

*S*cotland, *1864*

AGONY.

That was all Jael could feel. But he didn't waste a single moment thinking about his physical pain. He needed to find his wife. Fear stabbed at him, but he brushed it away and concentrated on his tasks with his current limited capacity. Charmine was alone, strolling her beloved Scotland hillside. Nobody knew she was with him on this mission. He had thought she was safe.

That was until Luna and her evil army had ambushed him. They had wounded him, using their dark magic to cut off his power and sever his wings. They wanted to take his light. He was at the highest rank in the council of angel of light. Other angels would have died with humiliation. He would have terminated himself if this had happened before.

But not now.

He was no longer by himself. He had Charmine, and she was carrying their first child. He was a father, and he had a family to protect. Protecting his light was a matter of the greater cause. If he gave them the light, they would let him live to come back to his family. But if the evil possessed his light, that would mean the end of the many worlds he'd sworn to protect. Innocent people and creatures would be killed. Families would be broken. He needed to survive and protect the light at the same time.

There was only one way out of this—relinquishing his angelic power. Doing so had reduced him to an ordinary human in the original form in which he was born.

He would never forget the look of disappointment and anger on Luna's face. He had stood in front of her, an ordinary and injured man, looked into her eyes, and challenged her to kill him. He knew she wouldn't do it. She hadn't gotten what she'd come for. Killing him would be an acceptance of defeat, and she took failure poorly.

Not until she had roared in fury and run away had Jael realized she could have used their sisterly connections to find out that Charmine was with him. Now she would attack Charmine.

He looked down at his injured human body. He couldn't run fast. He couldn't fly. He had no power. Being human sucked.

"Don't be too disappointed, Jael. You're a good angel. I'd be happy to give you a second chance."

The voice came from behind him. Jael turned around and said, "I don't deal with Xiilok people, Arete."

Arete chuckled. He stood eight feet tall, and long white hair covered half of his face, making him look even more mysterious and evil than he already was. He looked to be in his fifties, in Earth age, but Jael knew they had both been in their thirties when they'd chosen their very different paths and parted a few hundred years ago. Jael had retained his same look for a long time. But time hadn't agreed as well with Arete.

"I thought angels held no prejudice against any creature," Arete said.

"I'm no longer an angel."

"I can see that."

"So why are you here? I can't help you. I can't even help myself right now."

"There is a way."

Jael raised an eyebrow.

Arete smiled. "Come with me to Xiilok and be my commander. You have skills. You don't need the power from the Gods."

"My skills were given to me by the house of Gods. Although I'm no longer an angel, I can't use those skills to serve the Gods' adversaries."

Arete laughed. "Oh no, I'm on your side this time. Luna is your enemy, and she is killing your wife right now."

Jael shifted his stance.

"I know we didn't part on good terms," Arete continued, "but I guarantee you that we are on the same side. You want to protect the light and your family from Luna, and I don't want Luna getting the light because she will become too strong for my liking. I don't need competition."

"How can I be sure you don't want the light for yourself?"

Arete shook his head. "The light doesn't work with my kind of dark magic."

Jael nodded. "All right, and you promise to help me save my wife now?"

Arete nodded. "Of course." Then he gestured Jael to follow him. Jael obeyed. Arete made it a few steps before Jael charged at him from behind. He pulled a knife from his boot, leaped into the air, and stabbed at Arete's head. Arete ducked, and the knife cut off his left ear.

"You tried to stab me from behind!" he roared.

Jael cursed his human body. He wasn't used to such slow movement. "Normally, stabbing someone from behind sounds bad. But I'm at a disadvantage here."

"You don't need to protect the light for those who have sold you short. How do you think Luna got the information about your mission? Didn't you suspect a traitor in the house of Gods? Which is worse...a traitor or an adversary with good intentions?"

"Dead or alive, I will never betray the Gods. If Luna kills Charmine, her own blood sister, there is no good in your dark magic, regardless of what kind it is. You'll never have good intentions toward the light of Gods."

Arete swung his arms. A gust of wind picked up Jael's body, spun him in the air, and smashed him down to the ground. He heard the bones in his body rattle. He knew he would be dead soon. Arete walked over and stomped his foot down on Jael's chest, pinning him to the ground. "You're wrong this time, Jael. I do want to save Charmine. And only you can lead me to her."

"Why?"

Jael stomped his foot hard on Jael's chest, making him spit out blood. "Do not question me." He picked Jael up by the collar. "Find her, or she'll be dead."

While on the ground, Jael had grabbed the knife he had dropped. When Arete picked him up, he swung it and stabbed at him again, this time aiming for his heart. Quickly reacting, Arete's hand turned into a long blade. It pierced Jael's body from the front to the back. Arete pulled his steel hand out of Jael's body, letting him collapse to the ground.

Arete was so upset he slashed randomly at the tall grass. "I should have known. You'd die for those who betrayed you in a heartbeat. Your wife would do the same. Righteous parents. Virtuous child. If Luna can convert your child, it will become the best of all evils. The strongest." Arete hissed and growled. "We have to get to Charmine. I can't let Luna get the child," he said as he stomped around.

On the ground, Jael said, "I won't let you have my child..."

Then he closed his eyes and drifted off into oblivion. He heard thunder exploding. He felt the wind. He felt himself flying. Then he felt comfort. Something soft and warm wrapped around his body. It felt like he was being cradled by strong feathered wings. He heard a soothing female voice echoing from a distance, "You're a good angel, Jael. Hold on to your faith. You're not alone."

He tried to open his eyes, but all he saw was whiteness.

THIS IS THE END OF
OLEANDER - DARK SOLAR - BOOK 1
PLEASE TURN TO THE NEXT PAGE FOR SAMPLE CHAPTERS
OF
WOLFSBANE - DARKSOLAR 2

SAMPLE CHAPTERS

DARK SOLAR TRILOGY
by D.N Leo

OLEANDER
WOLFSBANE
MAIKOA

Dark Solar Trilogy - By D.N. Leo

PROLOGUE

*S*cotland, *1864*

JAEL STARED at the bloodstains on what used to be the peaceful Scottish greenfield. The grass had been killed by venomous fumes, which Jael was sure were coming from Luna, the dark magic sorceress. And the bloodstains belonged to Charmine, his newly wedded wife.

The scent of Charmine mixed with her blood and the ashes from the burned bush made his hands shake, his knees weaken, his heart race with fear, and his blood boil with rage.

Jael straightened up his body. He couldn't afford a mistake right now. He couldn't let himself be weak. God had given him a second chance to live and reclaim his angel power. God wouldn't have sent him back here just to see he had failed his family. God wouldn't save his life just to let him learn he had let Charmine and their stillborn first child die at the hands of evil.

He traced his fingertips over the bloodstains. So much blood . . . but his wife was a fighter. He was sure she had survived this attack from her evil sister. *Where are you, Charmine?* His eyes desperately scanned the hillside.

He searched every inch of the vista, using every ounce of his energy along with the light source he had. He found nothing but trails of blood. Then, in the dead grass, he saw a leather-bound book covered in bloodstains. He picked it up. It was a fairy tale Charmine had just bought in town.

He had observed her from a distance as she went into the bookstore. He felt uneasy when she mixed in among humans in the middle of a crowded town. He didn't mind humans, but he disliked the supernatural creatures walking among them. The stray creatures were unpredictable, dangerous, and had a minimal sense of morality.

Jael kept at a distance to give Charmine some space. As an apprentice in the house of Gods, she rarely traveled to the outside world. Thus, whenever he had a chance, he took her on a mission with him. Earth was her favorite place in the cosmos.

When she left the busy town for the peaceful hillside, he had thought it was safe and had gone about his mission. That was one of the rare mistakes he had made in his life, and he could only hope it hadn't cost him his family. He was the angel of light with the highest ranking in his council. He was the one who gave hope to his subjects —those he had sworn to protect. Now, when he needed hope, he wasn't sure from whom he could ask it.

As the thought enraged him, he heard a noise from a large pile of charred grass. He darted over to it and yanked out a small creature. It had been wounded and burned so badly that he couldn't tell what species it was. Judging by its charred skin and what was left of its face, the creature wouldn't last long.

"What are you? Where are your people?" Jael asked without expecting a coherent answer. The creature looked like an elf. If so, it might have enough supernatural power to heal itself if he gave it some help.

He straightened the head of the creature, trying not to cause more damage to its badly damaged skin. The creature's pointy left ear moved slightly, and it opened its two eyes that glowed like two large green lightbulbs. While its ears made it look like an elf, its eyes were certainly not those of an elf.

"Take it easy. If I give you some light, like a power source, would it help? I don't want to push the light in if your body will reject it."

The creature uttered a barely audible sound. "Please," it said.

Jael nodded. He held the creature's small hands and gently pushed some light energy into its body. In a short moment, its green eyes blinked and then opened wide, looking even larger than they did before. Some of its burned patches of skin started to heal. The healthy skin began to change from a shade of orange to light green and then to a deep blue.

"You're a sea-elf!" Jael gasped. "How did you get up here? Let me take you back to the water."

"No, I'm human."

"What?"

"She made me."

"She? Do you mean Luna?"

The creature nodded. "She took the heart of something at sea and put it inside me . . . just to keep it beating."

"She ripped your human heart out?" Jael asked but didn't need an answer. He knew what Luna had done. It was a ritual in dark sorcery to create supernatural creatures she could control. He had always thought it was a myth. Jael asked, "Did she . . . curse someone?" and this time, he didn't wish for an answer.

The creature closed its eyes, and in a short moment, its face started to form into the shape of a young man, but as it did, its heartbeat weakened, and its breathing started to labor.

"She changed you. You're not meant to be on land. You'll die," Jael said.

"I'd rather die than live like this."

Jael said nothing. He picked the man up in his arms, spread his wings, and flew toward the water.

"You're an angel!" the man whispered.

"Yes, but I can't bring you back from death. God created you, and it's your decision to keep your life or not. But nobody has the right to take life or your heart away from you."

"If you had come earlier, you could have saved her."

Something inside him broke. It might have been his heart. Flying against the strong wind, he looked down and asked the man, "Did you see Luna kill my wife?"

"Oh ... oh dear God, that was your wife? No, she fought hard. She didn't die. She killed Luna. And as you can see, Luna burned every-thing before she died."

"So why did you say I could have saved my wife if I'd come earlier?"

They had arrived at the coastline. Jael put him down close to the edge of the water. The man was weakening every second he drew in air. Jael dragged him into the water.

"Angel, what is your name?"

"I'm Jael. I am the angel of light."

"I want to die as a man."

"Not on my watch. I can't let you do that."

"Luna cursed your child before she died."

Jael stopped breathing for a second. "With what?"

"She planted the heart in me and took me to the hill. I heard her chanting a spell, and I think she wanted to place this heart into your wife's body after she cursed your child to have no heart. She was going to rip the heart out of your wife and replace it with this one ..."

Jael stopped dragging the man to deep water. The man stood up as he had now regained some strength.

"She cursed our child?"

"Yes, I'm so sorry. Your wife killed her after that. But the curse had been completed."

"Did you see where my wife went?"

The man shook his head. "No, but she didn't go by herself. She was hurt badly. Someone took her, and I saw its shadow. Whoever or whatever it was, it was very large. I couldn't see much. I'm sorry. It might have wings ... just like yours. But I don't think it was an angel."

"Why?"

The man looked at Jael. "Because angels don't rip someone's heart out with their bare hands. That thing took Luna's heart. Then it grabbed your wife and vanished."

Jael nodded. "You should go."

The man bowed. "I owe you my life," he said then dove into the water and swam away.

Jael looked to the horizon where the water met the sky. He swore to bring Charmine and their child home. He was an angel, and he had been protecting his subjects without fail for more than a hundred years. Now, the most important subjects in his life were in trouble. If he failed to save his own family, wouldn't it defeat the whole purpose of God creating him?

Among those at the same rank, he was the best of them all. In a hundred years of battle, he had lost only once. And that loss was to the person who had just taken Charmine.

CHAPTER 1

Dinah walked around the exclusive chemical lab at the headquarters of LeBlanc Pharmaceuticals in London. It had been three days, and she hadn't been able to develop the compound Ciaran had asked her to make. In Iilos, she would have blamed limited resources. She looked around and sighed. Any government in the cosmos would be drooling just to get their hands on this lab. The slow process could be because she had never before made weapons of this caliber. Or maybe she wasn't as good as she had thought and should settle for being a private investigator rather chemical engineer. But damn it, she *liked* chemistry.

Dinah frowned and rubbed her thumb on the button of the weaponry jacket Ciaran had made for her. He always asked for two-hundred percent commitment from those who worked for him. He wasn't king of the most prosperous universe in the multiverse for no reason.

A week ago, Earth time, Arete had challenged Ciaran, his council, and Arik to the second round of the multiversal hologame. Xiilok rebels had used a toxic fume that had nearly killed Ciaran and Madeline, and Ciaran believed they'd use an even more lethal weapon against them in the game. He wanted Dinah to create a compound that would protect them and prevent them from being affected.

"Piece of cake! I'll just pull the formula out of my ear," she said to the computer monitor which was streaming out test results that amplified the magnitude of her failure.

She raised her arms in the air in frustration then let them fall at her sides. Turning around, she walked straight into a trolley at the corner of the room, sending lab tubes and equipment shattering all over the floor.

"Ow!"

She had bumped her hip on the side of the trolley. She wasn't clumsy, but her frustration with the task at hand had cause her to be careless.

"You're such a klutz, Dinah." Her business partner grinned from the doorway.

"I'm not in a good mood, Cooper!"

He sauntered in without an invitation and sat on her lab stool. She was only five foot two, so she had adjusted the height of the stool to suit her needs. Cooper readjusted it so that his lanky body could settle comfortably. "You won't be in a good mood being around Arik."

"Well, I'll need to use that chair soon because someone has to develop a chemical compound to protect us in the upcoming multiversal hologame."

"I've been working out all night. My muscles are screaming. Can I sit for a bit?"

Dinah wagged a threatening finger at him. "I made those fake ab muscles for you. Remember that I can take them back."

He gestured up and down his torso. "They're already gone . . . when Ciaran shot at me in the market, remember? But I'm happy with the way I look now. I work out just to improve my agility."

"Jenny and her martial arts have had some good influence on you then?"

"No one can influence me. I'm always comfortable in my own skin."

Dinah rolled her eyes. "Says one who begged for fake abdomen muscles a short while ago!"

"Come on, can we not talk about that?"

"Yes, sure, if you stop calling me a klutz."

"It's a deal. Listen, I'm here to ask you for a favor."

"Naturally." Dinah rolled her eyes again. "I won't make you a love potion."

"No, that's not what I need. But if I don't get this problem figured out, no love potion will help."

Dinah frowned. "Are you okay?"

Cooper shook his head. "I've been thinking about the sound I heard when I called you from Iilos and didn't get a response."

"You said it sounded like a space creature. And it made perfect sense because we'd just had a fight before that, and they took my communication unit."

"Yes, but hear me out. I don't think it's just any sound. It was a static noise, like someone was tuning for frequency from the multiverse."

"Yes, we knew that, Cooper. Arete and his people were searching for some kind of frequency, and they had been manipulating Arik's brain waves. That was why he heard crazy music and all that."

"Yes, but I thought about it again, and it's not that simple. Or maybe it is in Arik's case. But in my case, when I played that sound again and again in my head, it started to make some sense. If I rearrange some of the tune, it's like a song. And in my last attempt, I think I got it right."

Dinah raised an eyebrow.

He sighed. "When it formed some sort of sensible tune, it shot a shock wave through my body. The energy in me surged and then subsided." He stood up and looked at her. "Unfortunately, it stayed that way. At the subsided level."

"So you lack energy? You need a vitamin shot?"

He raked his hands through his hair. "It's not that kind of energy. It's my libido."

"Cooper! You have officially crossed the line of our business partnership! You want me to help you get your rocks off?"

"Lower your voice, Dinah. Come on!"

"Cooper, I know masculine performance is important for a man. But we're on a mission here. The multiverse is in trouble. Lives are at stake. And you're worried about your libido?"

"I'm the one who's making sacrifices for the greater good here, telling you about my manliness problem and all."

"How is that sacrificing?"

"I think the control from the badasses who are hunting for the apertures has something to do with chemicals and a mind-controlling frequency. But you know that much. I also think they tried to either control or get information about something much more primal than that. Like sexual urges. I mean, think about it. In one sequence, my libido is up. Reversing it, my libido is down. And that was controlled across the cosmos."

Dinah nodded. "They're trying to control senses." She paced the room. "This is bad. Really bad. Senses rely on the immediate environment, and that's impossible to formulate without extensive simulation. That's beyond my skill set. But Ciaran can do it."

"Wait, you're not going to tell Ciaran about my libido problem, are you?"

"How else am I going to explain about the controlling of energy via multiversal frequencies?"

"Just say energy . . . or senses."

"Yes, but sexual urges are a primal sense. Those urges control human beings in a lot of ways. What if we miss out on the bigger picture by omitting that information?"

"I don't know . . ." Cooper said in frustration.

"It looks like we're having a heated debate about lab results?" Ciaran said from the doorway.

CHAPTER 2

Arik hunched down at a desk in the private apartment block of LeBlanc Pharmaceutical headquarters. He had been here before—during the time he buddied up with Ciaran and everyone else in the LeBlanc family. His mind wandered back to the time when things fell apart—he knew Ciaran had deliberately put him in this corner to prevent him from encountering staff.

He was supposed to trace back to the time he'd met the Xiilok people and figure out how Arete had played with the multiversal frequency of his brain waves. Ciaran bet Arete hit randomly at anyone who was prone to the signals.

But what would Arete's endgame be?

Arik wanted to pace the room but thought better of it, so he stayed focused on the task at hand. He was taking notes of all possible events and incidents around the time he met the yellow shield tribe in Xiilok.

Arik wasn't into computer games, let alone the multiversal hologame. He barely comprehended the concept. The multiverse was Ciaran's turf. Arik thought he could contribute in a small way by recalling and recording exactly what had happened the day he first saw the aperture. But bad memories plagued his mind and kept breaking his concentration. He closed his eyes to rest and leaned back in the chair. The clock on the wall teased.

Tick tock.

Tick tock.

It was as if the clock was counting down the time left until the multiversal hologame challenge.

He thought he had settled in as a professor at Oxford University, living his own quiet life. Apparently, someone or something out there in the cosmos didn't accept his life of peace.

He turned around, responding to a gentle knock at the door, and saw Dinah. The sight of her always refreshed and brightened his mood, no matter what his state of mind.

He still chuckled to himself when he thought about the first time they met when she had somersaulted into his lecture theater, struck a spectacular pose upon landing, flung one high-heeled red shoe at him, and unintentionally ejected one of the wings in her weaponry suit.

It had only been a short time since they'd met, but he found it hard to imagine life—after this multiversal attack event was over and he had to go to Xiilok—without Dinah in it. He'd gotten used to seeing the fragile, porcelain skin on that foxy oval face, and her pouting lips, especially when she tried to tease him or when she disagreed with him. He loved the long, black hair that wrapped around her shoulders. He was sure she intentionally brushed his skin with it whenever she walked past him, jolting his system with inexplicable sensation.

"Dinah." He smiled.

She entered the room graciously. Arik reached over and pulled a trolley of books he had just ordered from the university aside because he had some odd feeling that Dinah would bump into that hard object on her way in.

"If Ciaran has sent you, no, I haven't anything for him."

She smiled. "Yes, Ciaran sends me. But no, he didn't expect you to have anything done yet. We have a change of plans."

"Why can't he talk to me himself?"

"He was about to, but I asked if I could talk to you first."

Arik raised an eyebrow, waiting. As Dinah moved closer to him, he felt a wave rush through his body. There was nothing wrong with being attracted to a beautiful woman, but the timing was poor. Arik shook his head to clear the thoughts out of his mind.

"Why not?" Dinah asked.

"I'm sorry, what did you just say?"

"I said we should have a clear plan before you enter Mon Ciel because the history you have with Ciaran might mess with your head."

"It is now!" he muttered.

"What?"

"Never mind. So I guess Ciaran wants me to enter Mon Ciel to retrieve some information from Juliette?"

Dinah nodded.

"Why can't he do it himself? Do you know how sacred that palace is to his family?"

"He told me they have very strict security, and that he'll have to ask someone to take you in. You might know that the place is protected by a multiversal frequency shield designed to prevent any creatures from the multiverse entering."

"I know now." He sighed. "Ciaran and Madeline are Eudaizian now. That means they can't get into their own home. What a twisted fate!" Arik leaned back in his chair.

"Well, you might not be able to enter after you officially become a Xiilok tribe leader. But you're still human now, so we have a small window. But that's not why I'm here."

Arik approached. Dinah was small, and the top of her head barely reached his chest, so he lifted her up and sat her on the desk. He bent down, bracing his hands on the edge of the desk, and looked into her beautiful dark eyes. She blinked at him, and a tiny lash dropped onto her cheek. Her lips pouted slightly and parted as if inviting him to do the unthinkable.

"So why are you here? Hit me with the naked truth."

He felt as if he was outside his body, seeing himself approaching a woman without permission—the type of behavior he would only dare if he wanted a slap across the face. Or the type of thing he would have done when he was much younger.

"Arik!" she whispered with her mouth next to his ear.

"Yes," he said and turned. His lips almost touched the nape of her neck. He could feel the lust pulsing inside his body as he brushed his lips against her smooth skin.

"Arik!" she called out softly.

"Yes, Dinah!" He was going to kiss that skin.

"You're too close."

His surge of energy was brought to an abrupt halt. He jerked back, panting. "I'm sorry. I don't know why I did that." He felt out of breath and slightly dizzy.

Dinah held his shoulders. "Take it easy, Arik. That's why I'm here. And that's what I need to talk to you about."

He nodded and sat down.

Dinah continued. "In a nutshell, Ciaran believes that Juliette was working on an exotic compound before she died. And that compound might be the essential base for what I am trying without success to develop now. We don't have much time left before the challenge. So the quickest way to prepare is to get Juliette's formula, and I can work from there."

"What's the big deal here, Dinah? I can go in and grab the potion you need from Mon Ciel."

"There are two things you need to be aware of. First, Juliette didn't have the compound completed. Otherwise, Ciaran would have known. She did have the ingredients, though, and only you might be able to tell what they are."

"Me? I don't know anything about chemical compounds."

"But you do know Juliette."

Arik snorted. "Not well enough apparently."

"You were connected. Both you and Ciaran once loved that woman. And because of that connection, you will be able to tell."

"Because?"

"Because Juliette practiced alchemy."

"What?"

"Yes. Compounds or potions created from that practice have spiritual meanings that only connected people can read. And to connect back to the path of mind, you have to open up your feelings for Juliette. It' will be like opening up an old wound, and it will hurt."

Arik looked away, out the window for a moment. Then he turned back to Dinah. "All right. I can handle that. What's the second issue?"

Dinah smiled. "That's what Ciaran said. You can handle the first issue easily. The second one deals with your own emotional energy."

"Emotions again? Are you guys psychoanalyzing me like I'm a woman?"

"That's sexist, Arik."

"I'm sorry. Go on."

"You know you're prone to the multiversal frequency for some unknown reason. When you are opening up to connect with Juliette's past practice, you will be most vulnerable. Cooper had played with the frequency just a bit, and it affected his . . . let's call it his masculine performance."

Arik raised an eyebrow.

Dinah continued. "He's fine now. But he can detach the frequency from his mind, control it, and analyze it because we are not human. You are human, and you can't do what Cooper did. So if the frequency influences you, or if Arete is playing any tricks when you're in Mon Ciel—"

"I'm going cuckoo."

"Yes. And I am one hundred percent sure insanity is the result of being attacked by the multiversal frequency when opening your human emotion channels to the unknown. I don't know much about human emotions, but I'm an expert in multiversal mixed chemistry and brain waves. I know what it can do to you."

Arik paced back and forth then returned to Dinah. "So does Ciaran want me to go in or not? Why did he send you?"

"He is very sure you will accept the task if he asks you."

"Cocky bastard."

"He sent me to tell you that you have every opportunity to say no. This is not your war. And he will totally understand if you decline."

Arik approached Dinah and tilted her chin up to look into her eyes. "What do you think, Dinah?"

"I don't have an opinion on this because my mind doesn't work the same way. I know life and death, but I can't judge what it's like to lose your mind. With my makeup, it will never happen to me. But judging by how concerned Ciaran was about this, I'm saying you should decline. Also, I think you and Ciaran should decline the game, too. The most the both of you will lose is your bet."

"The bet is the Earth's population, Dinah."

"Yes, it's a lot of creatures to lose. A big bet. But you'll be the tribe leader in Xiilok. And Ciaran is king of Eudaiz, the most prosperous universe in the multiverse. Your lives are precious. Earth is only a small planet."

"You don't get it, Dinah."

"No, I'm sorry, but I don't. If the multiverse is at war, there will be losses and sacrifices. I don't understand how, when you and Ciaran got tangled up with the human issue, your great minds stopped working objectively."

"Because we're human. Regardless of whomever or whatever we might become, we were born and raised as human. Thus human interests will always be our priority."

Dinah nodded. "So what are you saying?"

He looked into her eyes and said, "I'm in."

CHAPTER 3

Madeline stepped out of the car and looked at the magnificent Mon Ciel, a palace resting imposingly on a hilltop in the exclusive area of Henley-on-Thames. The place had belonged to the LeBlanc family for a long time and bore many marks of their legacy. For her, this was the home that held many memories of Ciaran and her, of their relationship and how they had become soul mates.

The chilly breezes crept inside her jacket and made her shudder. Feeling a warm coat wrapped around her shoulders, she turned around and smiled at the sinfully handsome face of her husband—a face God had created when he was in the mood to forgive all mortal sins.

His striking gray eyes smiled back at her. "You're cold, first councillor."

Every time he called her first councillor, she wanted to swoon. But it didn't happen this time. A perk of being a mind reader was that she could occasionally peek into his mind, and those occasions tended to coincide with negative events—such as now.

A looming, dark cloud hovered over his mind. Deep concern about Arik's trip inside Mon Ciel was eating him up. Ciaran wasn't psychic, but he had excellent instincts. Whenever he sensed trouble that he could not fix, she saw those dark clouds in his mind. She made a mental note to do something about this when they returned to Eudaiz. She needed to train herself to see his mind when he was happy.

Behind them, other cars arrived and parked about one hundred yards away from Mon Ciel's fence. Arik, Dinah, Cooper, Jenny, and Lindsay exited these cars. This was a major event for people from the multiverse. However, because people on Earth were oblivious to it, Ciaran wanted to keep it low key.

Madeline entwined her fingers with Ciaran's and felt a slight squeeze from his hand. They both looked toward Mon Ciel. Not long ago, they'd fought supernatural creatures together, and Mon Ciel had been a safe haven for them. Now, looking at the palace from the outside, they saw a shield hovering over it like a dome.

The very shield that had protected them now prevented them from entering their own home.

Ciaran turned around. He rubbed his thumb over the dimple on her left cheek and smiled at her. "We have a new home now."

She nodded. "Yes, I love our new home. So whatever you do, make sure we return there. Our children are waiting."

"I'm sure we will." He kissed her lightly and turned toward the approaching group of people, leaving her standing there with a gigantic knot in her stomach.

Ciaran approached Lindsay.

Madeline recalled vividly the night she was attacked just outside London when Ciaran came to the rescue, a trip that had cost him his head of security and best friend's life. Lindsay was Ciaran's right-hand man at LeBlanc Pharmaceuticals. After that incident, he had tightened security and had always been there for Ciaran without fail. For Ciaran, Lindsay was more than just a subordinate. Lindsay was a friend—a part of his inner circle.

"I appreciate you helping me with this, Lindsay."

"Do you have to say that, Ciaran?"

"I understand it's difficult for you to escort Arik inside Mon Ciel given what happened in the past. But I don't trust anyone else to do this job."

"Understood."

Ciaran patted Lindsay's shoulder. "I owe you one."

"Don't mention it." Lindsay pulled out his cell phone and gave it to Ciaran. "Guard it with your life! My wife gave it to me." Lindsay grinned and returned to his car.

Ciaran walked toward Arik. "Once you're inside, I'll give you instructions on what to look for."

"How? Are you going to give me one of those fancy wrist units of yours?"

"No, it would be wiped clean when it goes past the protective shield. Lindsay has to leave his cell phone with me. You see?"

"Bloody hell, how much security do you need for a palace?" Arik exclaimed. Then he saw the look on Ciaran's face. "All right, I'll get in and out in one piece."

Ciaran nodded. "Thanks. I appreciate it. Once you're inside, Lindsay will get you a primitive piece of technology called a cell phone. Then I can call you from his phone and give you instructions."

"All right."

"Just to be sure, when you look at Mon Ciel now, you don't see a glowing, dome-shaped shield, do you?"

"Nope. It looks like just another castle in the English countryside. I'm not suicidal. If I saw the shield, I wouldn't put my neck through it. Trust me. Just out of curiosity, what would it do to you and other space creatures?"

"Electrocution. Burned toast. Barbecue. However you want to describe it."

"I get the picture."

Ciaran snapped a wristband onto Arik's wrist.

"Ouch!"

"If his band flashes, back the car right out. Don't go through the shield," Ciaran told Lindsay, who had settled into the driver's seat and started the car.

"Copy that."

The car moved slowly toward the gate, which automatically opened and cleared them in. Before the gate closed, Arik turned around and gave them a thumbs-up.

"Phew!" Cooper exhaled loudly.

Jenny chuckled. "I didn't know you cared about my brother that much."

"Oh, I don't. I'm just worried about the car."

Madeline wrapped her arms around Ciaran from behind. She didn't sense him feeling any easier. "What's wrong, Ciaran?"

"I don't know. I haven't figured it out yet."

From the corner of her eye, she saw Dinah looking anxiously at her wrist unit. She looked as agitated as Ciaran.

Ciaran's unit beeped, and he engaged immediately. "Talk to me, Jake."

Jake was head of intelligence in Eudaiz. He was very young to hold such an important position. But Ciaran trusted Jake's capability and integrity. Jake had proven Ciaran correct on several occasions.

"I'm calling you because the wristband you've used has been compromised. It's just been activated now, and it flashed on my screen."

Dinah rushed over. "What does that mean, Ciaran?"

"Which part was compromised, Jake?" Ciaran asked.

"The broadcasting function."

"It's going to broadcast manipulative frequencies!" Dinah teared up. "Can you call Arik now, Ciaran?"

Ciaran shook his head. "It's too late. I have to go in."

"Ciaran!" Madeline exclaimed although she knew Ciaran would ignore her.

He looked at Jake's image on the screen. "Send me TX25."

Jake's eyebrows shot up. "But it's a prototype."

"It's been tested. Park the capsule in the cross-dimension."

Ciaran's face hardened, and his eyes were as cold as steel. Madeline knew there was nothing she could say that would stop him from going inside. As she had done countless times before, she closed her eyes, concentrated, and forced her precognition and mind tracking abilities to work hard, hoping to find a solution.

CHAPTER 4

Arik's mouth hung agape for a moment when he saw the magnificence of Mon Ciel from the inside. In front of him were endless marble hallways, columns, decorative statues, and splendid works of art. But unlike other castles and palaces he had seen in England, behind the grandeur of Mon Ciel was a sense of home.

Now he understood why Juliette had no hesitation in calling this place home after she married Ciaran. He sighed. Dinah was right, opening old wounds was never easy. He should get past that state now. But for the purpose of the task at hand, he let the feelings linger.

He was supposed to channel Juliette's emotional energy. Normally, he would laugh at the ludicrous suggestion. But based on what had happened in the last few weeks, it might be the most sensible solution.

Something in his mind just clicked. It felt as if a pathway had been cleared. His mind's eyes saw a light at the end of the hallway. Whatever it was that Dinah had suggested seemed to work. Arik concentrated.

The light flickered a couple of times and then vanished. He shook his head and tried to relax, thinking about the palace and Juliette. The light appeared again.

"Arik!" Lindsay called out.

"Yes."

"We need to go and get the phone so Ciaran can give you instructions."

"Okay, you go. I'll stay right here," Arik said and focused on the light. He didn't want the vision to go away, and he was sure Lindsay didn't see it.

"I can't let you stay here by yourself. I promised Ciaran I'd get you out in one piece."

"No one's here. You think these marble statues are going to jump out and bite me? If you need to get the phone, go get it."

"Why can't you go with me? The equipment room is in the upper wing." Lindsay pointed toward the left.

Arik glanced to the right and saw the hovering light. "Where is Juliette's lab?"

"At the lower end." Lindsay pointed toward the light he couldn't see. "I can get you there after we get the phone. You need to talk to Ciaran because I don't have the code to get in."

"Right," Arik muttered and turned to follow Lindsay. But as soon as he turned, the light disappeared. "Oh no! Okay, how about I go to the lab now, and you go and get the phone."

"What's wrong with you? I told you I can't let you go to that wing by yourself."

"All right, why don't we go to the lab, and I'll see if I can figure out a way in and take the information myself. If I can't, then we'll come back for the phone."

"Why?"

"Can't tell you why. But I'm going to the lab now." Arik turned toward the right and walked along the corridor.

Lindsay muttered in protest but then followed.

Beside an imposing steel door was a keypad that glared at Arik in challenge. The light had taken him here, but it hadn't given him the code. Maybe he needed to go with Lindsay to the equipment room for the phone after all. A tingling sensation shot through this body, coming from the wristband Ciaran had given him. This must be one of Ciaran's tricks, giving him the code without telling him.

Arik stared at the keypad. A short moment later, the code illuminated on the keyboard. Arik followed the prompts. When he pressed the last digit, he heard a click, and the door slid open.

"Well, at least I didn't have to say open sesame," Arik muttered and entered the lab. Hundreds of colorful jars, tubes, and God knows what kind of lab equipment filled the room. Now he was seriously considering getting Ciaran's instructions. He squared his shoulders and concentrated.

He let his mind wander back to the time he and Juliette were lovers. It was a good time. He could see her beautiful face and flaming red hair. They were so young. She smiled at him. He remembered the vibrant energy that emanated from her body. She loved life, art, and nature.

He could see her walking through the field of wildflowers when they visited her hometown in Ireland. She inhaled the fragrance of the grass and flowers. She looked at them as if she knew them. She could talk to the wildflowers. She whispered something he couldn't hear.

"What's that, Juliette?" he asked.

She smiled and picked a bunch of wildflowers. "These are my favorite."

"Okay, let me get some more for you." He reached out to the flowers, and his hand hit a cold jar. He jerked his hand back, and the jar fell from his hand. Then his world went black. Soon after, he opened his eyes and found himself on the lab floor.

Lindsay held a jar of potion in his hand, looking at him with concern. "Are you okay? You just passed out and almost dropped this jar on the floor. I don't know anything about these potions. But I know we don't want to be near a broken jar."

Arik sat up. "Let me try again."

"Try what? Let's go get the phone."

"No, I have a sensation. Like a feeling of what might be the right potion. If we leave now, I'm not sure I can get that sensation back."

Lindsay nodded. "All right, I'll stay right here to make sure you don't break anything." Lindsay went and stood next to the door as if ready to jump out of the way if Arik broke anything in the lab.

Arik nodded and concentrated again. Images of Juliette flooded back to his mind—so fresh and so real. It felt like only yesterday that they were together.

He could feel his own movements in the lab. In a while, the memories seemed to subside. He didn't feel the need to remember or do anything more. His mind was flung back to reality.

He looked down at the lab table. Several jars of potions and powders were opened. There were signs of an experiment completed. He saw traces of colored powder on his hands. And he was holding a jar of liquid potion.

He knew this was the compound they needed. He stared at the light blue and purple liquid in the jar.

Then Arik felt a gun muzzle pressing against his temple.

"Put the jar down," Lindsay said.

WHAT'S NEXT

Dark Solar Trilogy is complete and released in e-book, audiobook
and print format.

You can order a copy of the next book here

DARK SORLAR TRILOGY HOMEPAGE

or
D.N. Leo's website
http://dnleo.com

EXCLUSIVE INVITATION

For a limited time, D.N. Leo gives away
e-books & audiobooks in the Multiverse Collection

CLICK THE LINK AND CLAIM YOUR BOOKS
http://dnleo.com

ALSO BY D.N. LEO

THE MULTIVERSE COLLECTION
SERIES READING ORDER

http://dnleo.com

A SHADE OF MIND

The Journey from Earth to Eudaiz

Main Characters: Ciaran, Madeline, Tadgh, and Jo

(Recommended reading in order)

1-4 Random Psychic

2-4 Forever Mortal

3-4 Elusive Beings

4-4 Imperfect Divine

—

MINDSCAPE TRILOGY

Main characters:

Ciaran, Madeline, Tadgh, Jo, Kyle, Hoyt, Ayana, Pete, Sizx, Lorcan, Orla

(Recommended reading in order)

Queen & Knight

Castle and Bishops

King's Endgame

—

SPECTRUM OF MAGIC

Main characters: Lorcan, Orla, Roy and Mori

(Recommended reading in order)

Spell Breaker

Fate Shifter

Cursed Stone

Magic Unborn

—

DARK SOLAR

Main characters:

Main characters: Dinah, Arik, Ciaran and Madeline

Oleander

Wolfsbane

Maikoa

SHADOW HUNTER TRILOGY

Fire at Crossroad (prequel)

Shadow Seeker

Shadow Keeper

Shadow Destroyer

BLOODSTONE TRILOGY

Ash of Scorpio (prequel)

Light of Demon

Shadow of Angel

Shade of Darkness

SILVER BLOOD

Main characters:

Ciaran, Madeline, Tadgh, Jo, Caedmon, Sedna, Roy, Mori, Zach, Mya, Lorcan and Orla

This series can be read in ANY order within the series and in related to other series.

Virgo

Libra

Scorpio

Pisces

THE GOOD DEITY

Main characters:

Main characters: Mya Portman, Zach Flynn, Leon, Kirra.

This series can be read in ANY order within the series and in related to other series.

Almost Countable

Almost Sure

Almost Everywhere

AFTERWORD

Thank you for reading.

If you enjoyed reading **Oleander - Dark Solar Trilogy - Book 1**, I would appreciate it if you would help others enjoy this book, too.

Recommend it. Please help other readers find this book by recommending it to friends, readers' groups and discussion boards.

Review it. Please tell other readers why you liked this book by reviewing it wherever you purchase the book from. If you do write a review, please send me an email at info@dnleo.com so I can thank you with a personal email.

OLEANDER
DARK SOLAR TRILOGY
BOOK 1

www.ingramcontent.com/pod-product-compliance
Lightning Source LLC
Chambersburg PA
CBHW072354020726
47506CB00004B/1108